SLAPPY BIRTHDAY
TO YOU

GOOSEBUMPS®
HALL OF HORRORS

#1 CLAWS!
#2 NIGHT OF THE GIANT EVERYTHING
#3 SPECIAL EDITION: THE FIVE MASKS OF DR. SCREEM
#4 WHY I QUIT ZOMBIE SCHOOL
#5 DON'T SCREAM!
#6 THE BIRTHDAY PARTY OF NO RETURN!

GOOSEBUMPS® WANTED:
THE HAUNTED MASK

GOOSEBUMPS®
MOST WANTED

#1 PLANET OF THE LAWN GNOMES
#2 SON OF SLAPPY
#3 HOW I MET MY MONSTER
#4 FRANKENSTEIN'S DOG
#5 DR. MANIAC WILL SEE YOU NOW
#6 CREATURE TEACHER: THE FINAL EXAM
#7 A NIGHTMARE ON CLOWN STREET
#8 NIGHT OF THE PUPPET PEOPLE
#9 HERE COMES THE SHAGGEDY
#10 THE LIZARD OF OZ

SPECIAL EDITION #1 ZOMBIE HALLOWEEN
SPECIAL EDITION #2 THE 12 SCREAMS OF CHRISTMAS
SPECIAL EDITION #3 TRICK OR TRAP
SPECIAL EDITION #4 THE HAUNTER

GOOSEBUMPS®

Also available as ebooks

ALSO AVAILABLE:

SLAPPY BIRTHDAY TO YOU

R.L. STINE

SCHOLASTIC INC.

Goosebumps book series created by Parachute Press, Inc.
Copyright © 2017 by Scholastic Inc.

ISBN 978-1-338-06828-3

10 9 8 7 6   17 18 19 20 21

Printed in the U.S.A.   40
First printing 2017

SLAPPY HERE, EVERYONE.

Welcome to My World.

Yes, it's *SlappyWorld*—you're only *screaming* in it! Hahaha.

Readers Beware: Don't call me a dummy, Dummy. I'm so wonderful, I wish I could *kiss* myself!

(But, hey, I might get splinters!)

I'm so great, I give myself *goosebumps*. Do you know the only thing in the world that's almost as handsome as my face? That's right—my face in a mirror! Haha.

I'm good looking—and I'm generous, too. I like to share. Mainly, I like to share frightening stories to give you chills—and make you do the Slappy Dance.

Do you know how to do the Slappy Dance?

That's right—you shake all over! Hahaha!

The story you are about to read is one of the most *awesome* stories ever told. That's because it's about ME! Haha.

1

And it's about a boy named Ian Barker. It's Ian's birthday and, guess what? He's having a party. At the party, Ian gets a present he thinks he's going to love.

Wouldn't you know it? The gift turns out to be a bit of a nightmare! Isn't that a *scream*?

Sure, it's Ian's birthday—but *I'm* the one who takes the cake! Hahaha!

Go ahead, readers. Start the story. I call it ***Slappy Birthday to You***!

It's just one more terrifying tale from SlappyWorld!

On Ian Barker's twelfth birthday, he received a gift that brought pain and terror to him and his entire family.

But let's not get ahead of ourselves.

Let's try to enjoy Ian's birthday for as long as we can. Just keep in mind that it was not the birthday Ian had hoped for. In fact, it quickly became a day he would have given anything to forget.

Ian came down to breakfast on that sunny spring morning, eager for his special day to begin. Almost at once, he had trouble with his nine-year-old sister, Molly. But that was nothing new. If you ask Ian, "How do you spell *Molly*?" He'll answer, "T-R-O-U-B-L-E."

Since blueberry pancakes were Ian's favorite, Mrs. Barker had a tall stack of them on the table. Ian and Molly ate peacefully for a while. Molly liked her pancakes drowned in maple syrup, and she used up most of the syrup before Ian had a chance. But Ian didn't complain. He was determined to be cheerful on his birthday.

But then they came down to the last pancake on the platter. When they both stabbed a fork into it, that's when the t-r-o-u-b-l-e began.

"Mine," Ian said. "You've already had six."

"But I saw it first," Molly insisted. She kept her fork poking into her side of the pancake.

"It's my birthday," Ian reminded her. "I should get what I want today."

"You *always* think you should get what you want," Molly declared. Molly has wavy red hair and blue eyes, and when she gets into an argument about pancakes—or anything else—her pale, lightly freckled cheeks turn bright pink.

Their mom turned from the kitchen counter. She had been arranging cupcakes on a tray for Ian's birthday party. "Fighting again?"

"We're not fighting," Molly said. "We're *disputing*."

"Oooh, big word," Ian said, rolling his eyes. "I'm so totally impressed."

They both kept their forks in the last remaining pancake.

"You're a jerk," Molly said. "I know you know that word."

"Don't call Ian names on his birthday," Mrs. Barker said. "Wait till tomorrow." She had a good sense of humor. Sometimes the kids appreciated

4

it. Sometimes they didn't. "Why don't you split the pancake in two?" she suggested.

"Good idea," Ian said. He used his fork to divide the pancake into two pieces.

"No fair!" Molly cried. "Your half is twice as big as mine."

Ian laughed and gobbled up his half before Molly could do anything about it.

Molly frowned at her brother. "Don't you know how to eat, slob? You have syrup on your chin."

Ian raised the syrup bottle. "How would you like it in your hair?"

Mrs. Barker turned away from the cupcakes and stepped up to the table. "Stop," she said. "Breakfast is over." She took the syrup bottle from Ian's hand. "You're twelve now. You really have to stop all the fighting."

"But—" Ian started.

She squeezed Ian's shoulder. "Your cousins are coming for your party. I want you to be extra nice to them and don't pick fights the way you always do."

Ian groaned. "Vinny and Jonny? They always start it."

"Ian always starts it," Molly chimed in.

"Shut up!" Ian cried.

"Just listen to me," Mrs. Barker pleaded. "I want you to be nice to your cousins. You know their parents have been going through a tough time. Uncle Donny is still out of work. And Aunt Marie is getting over that operation."

"Could I have a cupcake now?" Molly asked.

Ian slapped the table. "If she has one, I want one, too."

"Have you heard a word I said?" their mom demanded.

"I swear I won't start any fights with Jonny and Vinny," Ian said. He raised his right hand, as if swearing an oath. Then he stood up from his seat and started toward the cupcake tray.

"Hands off," Mrs. Barker said. "Go get your dad, Ian. Tell him the guests will be arriving soon."

"Where is he?" Ian asked.

"In his workshop," his mom answered. "Where else?"

"Where else?" Molly mimicked.

Ian walked down the back hall to the door to the basement. He thought about Jonny and Vinny.

Jonny and Vinny lived just a few blocks away. Jonny was twelve and Vinny was eleven, but they looked like twins. They were both big bruisers. Tough guys, big for their age, loud and grabby, with pudgy, round heads, short-cropped blond hair, and upturned pig noses.

At least, that's how Ian described them. The kind of guys who were always bumping up against

6

people and each other, always giggling, always grinning about something mean. Mean guys.

"They're just jealous of you." That's what Mrs. Barker always told Ian. "They're your only cousins, so you have to be nice to them."

Ian opened the basement door and went down the stairs two at a time. The air grew warmer as he reached the basement, and it smelled of glue.

Under bright white ceiling lights, his father stood hunched over his long worktable. He turned as Ian approached. "Oh, hi, Ian."

"Hey, Dad," Ian started. "Mom says—"

"Here's a birthday surprise for you," Mr. Barker said. He reached both hands to his face, plucked out his eyes, and held them up to Ian.

Ian groaned. "Dad, you've been doing that joke since I was two. It just isn't funny anymore."

Mr. Barker tossed the eyeballs in the air and caught them. "You love it," he said. He set down the eyes and picked up a tiny arm and leg from the table. "You'd give an arm and a leg to do the eye joke as well as I do."

Ian laughed.

He gazed at the pile of arms and legs and other body parts on the long worktable. Broken dolls were piled at the other end. Doll heads stared wide-eyed at Ian as he surveyed his dad's work area.

Dolls stared down from shelves along two walls. Headless dolls. Dolls with eyes or arms or legs missing. A bucket beside the worktable was filled to the brim with yellow, red, and brown doll hair. There were shelves of dresses and pants and shirts and all kinds of new and old-fashioned doll clothing.

Ian's dad had started his doll hospital before Ian was born. He spent most every day down here, repairing the broken dolls, replacing missing parts, painting fresh faces, making old dolls look new. Then he carefully wrapped them and sent them back to their owners.

He picked up a slender paintbrush and began dabbing pale pink paint on a doll head's gray cheeks. "This is a vintage Madame Alexander doll," he told Ian. "It's quite valuable, and when I received it, the face was completely rubbed off. So I—"

A hard knock on a door upstairs made him stop. Someone pounded the door four times, then four more.

"That's the front door," Mr. Barker said. "It must be your cousins. Go let them in." He squinted at the doll face and applied some more dabs with his paintbrush. "I'll be there in a few seconds."

Ian trotted up the stairs, then hurried down the hall toward the front door. He heard four more hard knocks. "I'm coming, I'm coming," he muttered.

Ian pulled open the front door—and let out a startled shriek as Jonny landed a hard-fisted punch in the middle of his face.

3

"OWWWWW!"

Ian shut his eyes and screamed as his entire head throbbed in pain. He felt a trickle of blood drip from his nose. Screaming again, he grabbed Jonny by the throat and began to shake him.

"Hey—stop! It was an accident! An accident!" Jonny cried.

Vinny tried to pull the two boys apart. But Ian swung his elbow and bumped him off the front stoop.

"I swear it was an accident!" Jonny insisted. "I was knocking on the door."

Mrs. Barker appeared. "Didn't you see the sign by the driveway? This is a No Fight Zone."

Ian let go of his cousin and, breathing hard, retreated a step. Jonny scowled, rubbing his throat. "An accident," he repeated.

"Ian, why is your nose bleeding?" his mom asked.

"It was an accident," Jonny said again. "I knocked on Ian instead of the door."

Mrs. Barker gave Ian a gentle push. "Go get some tissues. You don't want to bleed on your birthday cake." She stepped aside so Jonny and Vinny could enter the house. "No fights today, guys," she said. "Let's have a nice, peaceful party."

"What kind of tortilla chips do you have?" Vinny asked.

The question took her by surprise. "Tortilla chips?"

"Do you have nacho cheese?" Vinny asked. "Jonny and I didn't have breakfast."

The two large boys lumbered toward the kitchen.

"Do your parents let you have tortilla chips for breakfast?" Mrs. Barker asked, following them.

"They don't care what we have," Jonny said. "They sleep late. They just tell us to grab something."

Molly appeared outside the kitchen. "Yo, Molly. How's it going?" Vinny said. He reached out a big hand and mussed up her hair. He and Jonny laughed.

"I just finished brushing it," Molly grumbled.

"Looks awesome," Vinny said. He snapped his fingers over her nose.

"Owww! You jerk face." Molly punched him hard on the shoulder.

He grinned at her. "Hey, no fighting. It's Ian's birthday." He mussed up her hair with both hands.

Jonny pushed past them into the kitchen. "Whoa. Cupcakes!" he cried. He grabbed one off the tray and shoved the whole thing into his mouth.

"Any good?" Vinny asked. He slapped his brother on the back, and a big glob of cupcake came flying from Jonny's mouth and landed on the floor. Both boys broke into loud hee-haws.

"You two are a riot," Molly said.

Vinny grabbed a cupcake and bit off the icing. He put the rest of it back on the tray.

Mrs. Barker lifted the tray, swung it away from the boys, and carried it to the breakfast table. "Let's save the cupcakes till later," she said. "I have a chocolate ice-cream cake for Ian, too. His favorite."

"I hate chocolate," Vinny said. "It gives me diarrhea."

Molly rolled her eyes. "Thanks for sharing."

Ian returned to the kitchen with a wadded-up tissue stuck in one nostril. He had decided to force himself to be cheerful and ignore the punch in the face. He really wanted to get along with his cousins today.

"What's up with you guys?" he asked.

"Jonny had a little trouble in school," Vinny said. He patted his brother on the shoulder. "He got caught stealing. Do you believe it?"

Mrs. Barker gasped. "Stealing? Really, Jonny?"

"No way," Jonny insisted. "I didn't steal that

12

girl's iPad. I borrowed it. I guess she didn't hear me ask."

Mrs. Barker narrowed her eyes at Vinny. "Vinny, that's serious. Why are you grinning like that?"

Vinny shrugged. "Just grinning. You know. It's kind of funny."

"No, it isn't," Mrs. Barker said. She turned to Jonny. "So what happened?"

"No big whoop," Jonny replied. He avoided her eyes. "I returned it and everything was okay." He gave Vinny a hard shove. "Do we really have to talk about it?"

Vinny raised both hands in surrender. "Okay, okay. I was just saying . . ."

Jonny started opening cabinet doors. "Where are the tortilla chips, Aunt Hannah?"

"I thought I'd save them for lunch," she answered. "Why don't the three of you go play video games while I get things ready?"

Jonny grabbed another cupcake and jammed it into his mouth.

"I don't want to play with them," Molly said. "They cheat."

"We don't cheat. You just stink at it," Vinny said.

"Vinny, that's not a good thing to say," Mrs. Barker scolded.

"I could *beat* you if you didn't cheat!" Molly declared.

Vinny snapped his fingers over her nose. "Owwww!"

Mrs. Barker sighed. "Molly, stay with me and help me get the sandwiches ready. You three—get out of here. Go play with the PlayStation upstairs."

Ian pulled the tissue from his nose. "Mom? Is my nose swollen?" he asked.

"A little, maybe."

"It was an accident. Really," Jonny said. He turned and the two cousins followed Ian out of the kitchen.

"I seriously hate them," Molly said when they had disappeared upstairs. She rubbed her sore nose.

"Yes, they're difficult," her mom agreed. "But as I said before, they have a pretty tough life. They're your only cousins, so—"

"I know, I know," Molly said, rolling her eyes. "So we have to be nice to them. But why do they have to be such animals?"

Mrs. Barker didn't reply. She started to pull food from the fridge. Molly found the hamburger rolls and began to spread them on a platter.

The house was quiet for at least five minutes.

Then Molly and her mom heard a loud shriek. Shouts. Hard thuds and thumps on the ceiling above their heads. One heavy thud shook the ceiling light. More angry shouts.

"What's happening up there?" Molly cried.

She and her mom went running to the stairs.

The screams grew louder as they raced to Ian's room. "What's going on?" Mrs. Barker shouted. Mr. Barker had run up from the basement. He was standing in the bedroom doorway.

"A wrestling match," he reported, shaking his head. "Jonny and Vinny are playing keep-away with the controller."

"Well, don't just stand there, George. Stop them!" Mrs. Barker cried. "Hey, guys, come on. No fighting. No fighting!"

Jonny sat on top of Ian, crushing Ian's chest under his bulk. Vinny waved the PlayStation controller in one hand. Ian swiped at it. Missed.

All three boys turned when Mrs. Barker yelled at them.

"Ian is being a jerk," Jonny said.

"Get *off* me, you fat pig!" Ian cried, shoving Jonny with all his strength. "I can't breathe."

"Ian, don't call names on your birthday," his mom scolded.

"I told you they are animals," Molly said.

"You're not an animal," Vinny told her. "You're an *insect*."

"She's not an insect," Jonny chimed in. "She's insect *larva*."

"What exactly is the problem here?" Ian's dad demanded. "Can't you guys even play video games without fighting?"

Jonny finally climbed off Ian. "Ian won't play fair," he said.

"That's a lie," Ian said, rubbing his crushed ribs. "They are total cheaters. They want double turns." He grabbed for the controller, but Vinny tossed it across the room to Jonny.

"We don't have a PlayStation at home," Vinny explained. "So we should get double turns."

"That's totally stupid," Ian said.

The three boys all started shouting at once. Mr. Barker stepped between them in the middle of the room. "I know what," he said. "Let's go downstairs and do birthday presents."

"I hope you won't fight over *them*," Ian's mom said, sighing.

The boys grudgingly agreed. "But Jonny and I still get another turn on the game," Vinny insisted.

A few minutes later, they had gathered in the living room to give Ian his presents. Jonny and Vinny sprawled on the couch. Jonny grabbed a handful of peanuts from the bowl on the coffee table and tossed them one by one to his mouth. The ones he missed fell onto the carpet.

Molly sat by the fireplace, straightening her hair with both hands. Ian dropped down on the floor.

His dad handed him a box wrapped in red-and-white paper. "This is from Vinny and Jonny," he said.

"It's the best present ever," Vinny said.

"If you don't want it, we'll take it back," Jonny added.

Ian ripped away the wrapping paper. "Hey! Cool! A Star Wars robot!"

"It's BB-8," Jonny said. "It's remote-controlled. Totally awesome."

"He goes all around the room, and you can make him say stuff," Vinny said.

Ian started to pry open the box lid. "Hey, the box has already been opened." He raised his eyes to his cousins.

"Yeah, well," Vinny said. He shrugged. "Jonny and I played with it at home before we brought it. You know. We tested it out for you."

Ian narrowed his eyes at Vinny. "Tested it out?"

"Sorry. It got a little scratched," Jonny said. "Hope we didn't wear down the batteries too much."

"Well ... it's way cool," Ian said. "Thanks, guys."

Ian's dad appeared, carrying a long black leather case by its handle. Larger than a guitar case, it was battered and scratched and looked really old. Mr. Barker wore a wide, pleased grin. "I think you're going to be surprised by this one," he told Ian. "You've been waiting a long time for it."

Ian lowered the case to the floor. It had a layer of dust over it and smelled kind of stale. He snapped the double clasps. The heavy lid didn't lift easily. He had to push hard with both hands.

Inside the case, a wide-eyed figure grinned up at him. A ventriloquist dummy.

The dummy had a large wooden head with dark brown hair painted over the top. Big black eyes. The wood on his sharp nose had a small chip in it. His grinning mouth was painted bright red.

He was dressed in a shabby gray suit. His white shirt had a stain on the collar. His red bow tie was crooked. The brown leather shoes on his feet were scuffed.

"Wow!" Ian exclaimed. "Wow! A real dummy! Dad, you know I've been wanting one for years."

Ian's parents both grinned happily.

"Wow. This dude is kind of ugly," Ian said. "I mean . . . he looks like a bad boy. His face is almost . . . evil."

Mr. Barker reached down and helped Ian lift the dummy from the case. "His name is Slappy. There's an interesting story that goes with this dummy," he said.

18

Ian held the dummy in his lap. Jonny leaped off the couch, bumping the peanut bowl off the table, and made a grab for it. "Can I try him?"

"No way." Ian swung the dummy out of Jonny's reach. "Shut up and let my dad tell the story."

Jonny muttered something and slumped back to the couch. He and his brother exchanged shoulder punches. Vinny grabbed some peanuts off the floor and shoved them into his mouth.

"What's the story, Dad?" Ian asked.

Mr. Barker reached down and turned the dummy's head from side to side. "Well, someone sent Slappy to me for repair," he said. "His eyes were broken, and his head was coming loose, and his jacket was shredded in back."

"So he's a used dummy?" Molly asked.

"Oh, I think he's had a lot of owners," her dad replied. "Slappy is older than he looks."

"If someone sent him to you to be fixed, why did you keep him?" Ian asked.

19

"That's the strange thing," Mr. Barker replied. "The owner didn't send a return address."

"Weird," Ian muttered, shifting the dummy to his other leg.

"This is a valuable dummy," his dad said. "I thought the owner just forgot to tell me where to send it back. So I repaired Slappy, fixed him up as best I could. And I put him in the closet and waited. I waited a year, hoping to hear from the owner. But . . . no."

"They didn't write to you?" Ian asked.

His dad shook his head.

Vinny laughed. "Maybe they didn't *want* him back."

"Maybe because he's so ugly," Jonny added.

Mr. Barker scratched his head. "Beats me," he said. "Anyway, he's all yours, Ian. Now you can practice making him talk without moving your lips, and you can work up a good comedy act with him."

"Hey, thanks, Dad," Ian said. "Check out his eyes. I like the way they stare at you. They're so real."

Jonny jumped off the couch again, dove forward, and grabbed Slappy's arm. "Come on. Let me have a turn."

"Give me a break," Ian said. "I haven't even had a turn yet. Let go, Jonny."

"I just want to try him," Jonny insisted. "For a few seconds. Come on, you jerk."

"Everybody stop calling names," Mrs. Barker snapped. "I'm serious."

Jonny pulled the dummy's arm hard. Ian held Slappy tight around the waist. They had a short tug-of-war till Mr. Barker stepped up to them.

"Let go, Jonny," he said. "You're going to wreck him, and I just got him fixed up."

"Not fair!" Jonny insisted.

"Just give Ian a chance," Mr. Barker insisted. "He'll give you a turn later, won't you, Ian?"

"No," Ian said.

Jonny clenched his hands into fists and stomped back to the couch. He grabbed some peanuts from the floor and began tossing them one by one at Ian.

Ian ignored him. He raised the dummy higher on his lap and placed a hand on its back. "How does it work, Dad?" he asked. "How do you move his mouth? Does your hand go inside here?" Ian pointed to an opening in the dummy's back.

Mr. Barker nodded.

Ian pushed his hand into the opening—and Slappy screamed: *"Stop that, you fool! I'm ticklish!"*

Jonny and Vinny both cried out. Molly gasped and squeezed her hands to her face. Mrs. Barker's eyes went wide with surprise.

Ian laughed. "That was *me*—not the dummy. Did you really think the dummy screamed? I must be a pretty good ventriloquist!"

Mr. Barker patted Ian on the shoulder. "Very good. That was funny. You have to find a good personality for Slappy."

"Make him mean," Molly suggested. "He has that mean grin on his face. Seriously."

"*I hate your grin, too, Worm Lips!*" the dummy cried in a high, shrill voice.

Molly growled and punched Ian in the back.

"Hey, you said to make him mean!" Ian protested.

Molly rolled her eyes. "*You're* the dummy, Ian!"

"Hold on. I have a present for you, too, Molly," Mr. Barker said. "I always give you a present on Ian's birthday, don't I? So you won't feel left out."

"Where's *my* present?" Vinny grumbled.

Mr. Barker disappeared for a few minutes, then returned carrying a long box wrapped in silvery paper. He handed it to Molly, who ripped the paper off immediately. She pulled a tall, old-fashioned-looking doll from the box. The doll had red hair and a pretty pink face. She was dressed in a long blue ball gown under a flowing red cape. "Oh, wow. She's beautiful."

"It's a very old Patsy doll," her dad said. "These dolls were popular in the 1930s. Perfect for your collection, I thought."

"Oh, thanks, Dad." Molly said. "I love her. What should I name her?"

"How about Dumbo, like you?" Jonny suggested. He and his brother hee-hawed and bumped knuckles.

"I'm going to name her Abigail," Molly said.

"Abigail. I like it. That's a good old-fashioned name," Mrs. Barker said.

"Great presents," Ian said. He stood up, holding Slappy around the waist.

"Food time! Food time!" Vinny chanted. He and his brother jumped up from the couch. The floor was littered with peanuts. They stepped right over them.

Vinny grabbed Slappy. "My turn," he said. He grabbed the wooden hand and tugged.

Ian tried to swing the dummy away. "Let go, Vinny."

Vinny gave another hard tug—and pulled Slappy's hand off.

"You lamebrain!" Ian screamed.

Gaping at the dummy hand he held, Vinny backed away. "It was an accident. You saw it. It was an accident."

"You're going to be in an accident," Slappy cried. *"Your face is going to crash into my FIST!"*

Vinny growled and made a move toward Ian.

"I didn't say it! The dummy said it!" Ian exclaimed.

Everyone laughed.

How ridiculous.

SLAPPY HERE, BOYS AND GHOULS.

You have to *hand* it to Vinny. He sure knows how to ruin a birthday party.

Vinny and Jonny are the kind of cousins you want to have. They're the kind of cousins you want to have—a thousand miles away! Hahaha.

Of course, I can understand the boys fighting over me. If I weren't *me*, I'd fight over *me*, too! Hahahaha! I'm delightful. I'm de-lovely. I'm de-Slappy! Hahaha!

I didn't like it when Molly said I looked mean. It just isn't true. I don't have a mean bone in my body. That's because I don't have *any* bones in my body!

But, listen to me, readers: I'm a nice guy. If you don't believe me, I'll punch you in the face! Hahaha.

Anyway, I think Ian and I are going to be good friends. He waited a long time to get me.

Actually, he waited three years. But I'm worth the wait! Hahaha.

He first got interested in ventriloquist dolls on his ninth birthday.

Let's go back in time. Let's go back to Ian's birthday three years ago, and you'll see how it happened . . .

"Where are we going, Dad?" Ian asked.

Mr. Barker held the car door open. "Just get in," he said. "It's a birthday surprise. How could it be a surprise if I told you?"

Ian slid into the passenger seat and started to fasten the seat belt. He grinned at his dad. "I already guessed it. We're going to the video game tournament in Charleston."

"Wrong."

Mr. Barker backed the car down the driveway and headed toward the highway.

"SeaWorld?" Ian guessed. "We did that last year, remember? Molly made faces at the sharks?"

"Not SeaWorld," Ian's dad said. "Not any place you've been before. You want an adventure, right? You told me you want an adventure."

It was a bright spring morning. Sunlight danced over the windshield. The trees along the road shimmered with fresh green leaves.

"Come on, Dad, *tell* me," Ian insisted. "It's *my* birthday. And you know I hate suspense."

Mr. Barker chuckled. "You *love* suspense. What about all those scary books you read? And the frightening movies you watch? And the weird PlayStation games you play?"

Ian rolled his eyes. "Dad . . ."

"Okay, okay," Mr. Barker said. He slowed for a stoplight. "I'm taking you to a doll museum."

"Huh?" Ian's mouth dropped open. "You're joking, right? Like I'm really into *dolls*."

"Trust me, Ian. This isn't like all the other antique doll places I visit."

Ian fiddled with the seat belt. "Let me out now."

"Very funny. Just sit back and relax," his dad said. "Would I take you to a place you'd hate?"

Ian growled under his breath. "Where is it, anyway?"

"It's hidden on the edge of a large forest," Mr. Barker said. "It's called the Castle of the Little People. It's very hard to get in. The man who runs it is very strange. I've been trying for years. I think you and I will have quite an adventure."

Ian rolled his eyes. "Bor-ing," he said.

Later, Ian changed his mind.

The visit to the Castle of the Little People was far from boring. It turned out to be terrifying.

A few hours later, Mr. Barker pulled the car into the wide asphalt parking lot. Ian gazed out the windshield as a shadow rolled over the car.

The shadow of the Castle of the Little People.

"Dad, it must be closed," Ian said. "We're the only car here."

"Yes. It's closed today," his dad replied. "But I have an appointment with the owner."

Ian stared up at the dark stone castle with its twin towers and rows of black windows and slanting, black tile roof. The huge building rose over the trees like a giant creature guarding the forest behind it. Ready to pounce.

"It . . . it looks like a haunted house," Ian stammered.

Mr. Barker chuckled. "I *told* you it's your kind of place."

They climbed out of the car. Ian shivered. The air had suddenly turned cold. "Dad, there's no one here," he said. "The whole castle is dark."

"Stop being so tense," his dad said. "You're about to see some amazing creations."

The front entrance rose high above their heads. A brass door knocker poked out of the middle of the door. Mr. Barker banged it three times.

A few minutes later, the heavy door creaked open. Ian gasped at the figure in the doorway. A giant doll!

No. It took him a few seconds to realize he was staring at a tall man wearing a mask. A rubber baby-doll mask. It had curly blond hair at the top, rosy pink cheeks, and bright red lips in a pouty smile.

The masked man stepped forward. He was dressed in black and had a long black cape draped over his shoulders. Behind the mask, his eyes were a silvery gray. *Like metal*, Ian thought.

"Welcome to my castle," he said in a soft, whispery voice. "I am Dr. Klausmann."

"Thank you for seeing us when the museum is closed," Mr. Barker said. "This is my son, Ian."

The doll mask nodded up and down. "Please come in. And please pardon the mask. I'm afraid my face is unpleasant to look at. Actually, it gives people nightmares. I don't show my face to children."

Ian stared hard at the mask. He tried to imagine what Dr. Klausmann's face looked like. How ugly could it be? Could it really give nightmares?

Or was the castle owner joking . . . trying to make himself mysterious?

Ian and his dad followed the masked man into the large front entryway. It was dimly lit by flickering torches on the wall. Two hallways led in different directions. Each was guarded by a silvery suit of armor carrying a battle-ax.

Ian shivered. The air inside the castle was colder than the air outside. He heard a chittering, squeaky sound in the distance. Bats?

Dr. Klausmann led them to the hallway on the left. All the way down the hall, Ian could see glass display cases on both walls. They were brightly lit and appeared to be filled with dolls . . . Dolls posed in different scenes . . . dolls wearing safari clothes in a jungle scene . . . dolls in sailor suits on board a ship . . . dolls in ball gowns in a fancy ballroom . . . The displays glowed, making the hall as bright as day. The dolls stood alone or in groups of three and four, eyes wide and smiles bright.

"Because of my ugliness, I have surrounded myself with beauty," Dr. Klausmann said. He adjusted the baby-doll mask over his face as he led them slowly from display to display.

"I've never seen some of these dolls," Mr. Barker said. "They must be very rare—and very valuable."

"I hope you have not come to buy any dolls from me," Dr. Klausmann said, his voice muffled behind the mask. "These dolls are my family. I cannot sell my family."

"Ian and I are happy just to see them," Mr. Barker said.

They turned a corner. The dolls along this corridor were older. "Some of these are three hundred years old," Dr. Klausmann explained.

"And all in perfect condition," Mr. Barker added.

"Better than perfect," Dr. Klausmann said. "I've brought them to life!"

What does he mean by that? Ian wondered. He stifled a yawn. A bunch of old dolls. Big whoop.

Dad should have brought Molly here, he thought. Six-year-old Molly had already started her own doll collection.

Dr. Klausmann stopped. He leaned over Ian, the silvery eyes peering out from behind the baby-doll face. "Ian, I can read your mind," he said in his whispery voice.

"Huh?" Ian's heart started to pound. He didn't know what to say. This tall man towering over him, staring at him with that rosy baby face and those weird eyes . . .

How long do we have to stay here? he thought. And then he hoped Dr. Klausmann couldn't really read his mind.

"Follow me," Dr. Klausmann said, motioning them down another long hall. "I have something I know Ian will find fascinating."

Their shoes echoed off the hard marble floors. They passed a large glass case filled with doll heads. The heads were piled on one another, the eyes all staring through the glass.

Mr. Barker stopped to admire them. "I recognize some of them," he said. He pointed. "That one is very rare. Very valuable."

"I love pretty faces," Dr. Klausmann whispered. "My face is so ugly, my own mother couldn't bear to look at me. But these faces are all lovely to look at."

In the distance, Ian heard the shrill, chittering cries again. *If Dr. Klausmann likes pretty dolls, why does he keep them in this creepy castle?* Again, Ian hoped the man couldn't read his thoughts.

Dr. Klausmann pushed open a heavy wooden door at the end of the hall. He motioned for Ian to go in first. Ian stepped into a large, dark room. The air smelled stale and damp.

An enormous ceiling chandelier flashed on. Ian blinked in the bright white light. When his eyes could focus, he saw people sitting very still . . . dozens of odd-looking people on armchairs, sitting stiffly, gazing blankly . . .

"Ian, what do you think?"

Ian felt Dr. Klausmann's hand on his shoulder. As his eyes adjusted to the light, the seated figures became clearer. They were ventriloquist dummies. A roomful of them, on couches and stuffed into broad armchairs. Dozens more were propped up side by side along the back wall. They appeared to stare at him, wide-eyed, glassy-eyed . . . painted faces . . . ugly grins and hair standing up wild or plastered to the tops of their heads.

"My ventriloquist doll collection," Dr. Klausmann said. "Ian, are you impressed?"

Ian nodded. "They're awesome. They're totally freaky."

"They are my friends," Dr. Klausmann said. "Would you like to try one?"

Ian glanced at his dad. Mr. Barker was gazing from dummy to dummy, shaking his head in admiration.

"Whoa. Cool. Can I really try one?" Ian said. He followed Dr. Klausmann to an armchair in the front row. The doll collector lifted a dummy off the chair.

The dummy had black hair painted on its head. Its eyes were dark brown, and it had a dopey grin frozen on its freckled face, and a big front tooth poking out of its mouth.

The dummy wore a red-and-black flannel shirt under blue denim bib overalls.

"This is Farmer Joe," Dr. Klausmann announced. He motioned for Ian to sit down. Then he set the dummy down on Ian's lap. "Do you know how to control him?"

He didn't wait for Ian's answer. He pushed Ian's hands into the opening in the dummy's back. Ian fumbled till he found the controls.

"Go ahead. Try him out," Dr. Klausmann said. "Try to make him talk without moving your lips."

Ian made the dummy's mouth move up and down. "This is way cool," he said.

"Ian has always liked puppets," Mr. Barker said. "Remember those clown marionettes you had when you were younger?"

Ian nodded. He'd spent hours putting on puppet shows with those marionettes. He tilted the dummy on his lap and put on a funny voice: *"I'm Farmer Joe. I have to go milk the pigs now!"*

His dad and Dr. Klausmann laughed. "Very good, Ian," Dr. Klausmann said. "Feel free to explore the room. Try any dummy you'd like." He turned back to Mr. Barker. "Let me show you a few interesting things . . ."

Ian practiced moving Farmer Joe's mouth up and down. He moved his fingers until he found the control for the dummy's eyes. After a few tries, he could get the eyes to blink.

"I'm Farmer Joe," he said, keeping his teeth together, trying not to move his lips. *"Who are you staring at? Are you staring at me just because I need dental work?"*

He practiced working with the dummy for a few minutes. Then he placed it back on its chair and tried another one. This dummy was very dressed up in a tuxedo, white shirt, and bow tie. It had a black top hat on its head. Its shoes were shiny black leather.

"I'm Mr. Fancypants." Ian gave him a deep, throaty voice. *"I like to smoke cigars. But lighting a cigar is very dangerous since I have a wooden head!"*

Ian laughed, cracking himself up. "These dummies are more fun than marionettes," he told himself. "You can really make them come to life."

Next he tried a dummy with blond braids and big blue eyes. He named her Molly, after his sister, and he gave her a shrill, whiny voice. Ian gazed around the room. The dummies—dozens of them, all different—stared straight ahead. "Totally cool," he murmured.

He turned back to the front of the room. "Hey, Dad—look at this one." He bounced Molly the Dummy on his lap.

Silence. No reply.

"Hey—Dad?" Ian stood up and looked around the big room. "Dad? Where are you?"

He set the dummy down and took a few steps toward the door. He suddenly felt tense. His throat tightened. His hands were cold.

"Dad? Did you leave? You didn't say you were leaving. Dad?"

He knew he shouldn't be afraid. But he couldn't help it. The dummies had been fun to try. But he didn't really want to be left alone in this room with so many of them.

"Dad? Hey—Dad?" he called, his voice trembling.

He took a few more steps toward the door. Then he sensed something moving.

He turned back in time to see the dummies move their heads. All of them, all around the room. The dummies all tilted back their heads, opened their mouths, and began to laugh.

Ian gasped, staring in disbelief at the dozens of cackling dummies. Their mouths clicked and their cold, ugly laughter rang in his ears. He forced himself to spin away from them. He lowered his head and ran.

He shoved the door with both hands. It didn't budge.

Frantically, he pulled and pulled, and it finally creaked open.

Ian ducked into the dimly lit hall. He was standing at the very end. Squinting into the gray light, he called for his dad. "Where are you? Can you hear me?" His voice echoed off the stone walls.

Silence. No reply.

"Dad? Where are you?"

The only sounds were his ringing voice and the thuds of his pounding heartbeats.

He forced his legs to move and began to trot down the middle of the hall. This long corridor had no doors or windows, no brightly lit displays. He ran past solid gray walls. He felt as if he were running through an endless tunnel.

Ian stopped when the hallway turned. He found himself in another long corridor, this one lined with doll displays. "Dad? Are you down here?"

The dolls stared out at him from their glass cases. A weird forest scene was jammed with dolls with bear faces. They wore suits and dresses and stood on two feet, but their faces were furry, with long bear snouts. The next case showed angels with filmy wings and halos over their heads, flying in a cloudless sky.

"Dad? Hey—can you hear me?"

Ian's side hurt from running. He slowed to a walk as he made his way down this hall. It turned into another. He stopped.

Maybe I should go back. Maybe I should wait for Dad in the room with the ventriloquist dummies. He might be back there now, expecting to find me there.

But Ian realized he was completely turned around. He stood in the middle of this new hall, gazing one way, then the other. Which way? Which way?

He started walking again—and stopped at the end of the hall. Ian peered into a brightly lit glass office. A young woman sat at a desk, typing on a laptop. Ian saw posters of antique dolls on the wall behind her. A large brown teddy bear was propped up in a folding chair beside her desk.

She had short brown hair and was dressed in a dark blouse and jeans. She looked up and saw Ian staring in at her, and her mouth opened in surprise.

He stepped into her doorway.

"Can I help you?" she asked, her face still tight with alarm. "We are closed today."

"I know," Ian said. "I . . . I'm looking for my dad."

The young woman squinted at him. "Your dad?"

"Dr. Klausmann was showing us around," Ian explained. "And we got separated."

She studied him for a moment. "I'm sorry. Please repeat. *Who* was showing you around?"

"Dr. Klausmann," Ian said.

The woman frowned at him. "I'm sorry," she said. "There's no one named Dr. Klausmann who works here."

10

"Why don't you wait right here?" the woman said, standing up. "I'll have the security guard show you the exit."

I have to find Dad first, Ian thought. *There's something very strange going on in this museum.*

He spun around and ran back into the hall. He heard the woman shouting for him to stop. But he took off, running down the long corridor, dolls staring at him all the way.

Breathing hard, he turned a corner. And that's when he saw the figure in the far distance. So far down the hall, Ian could barely see him. "Dad?" Ian squinted hard, struggling to see.

The man was walking slowly, half hidden behind the haze of white ceiling lights. He walked steadily, arms down at his side.

Ian waited for him to come into focus. It had to be his dad. *Had* to.

But why was he walking so slowly?

"Dad? Here I am. Dad?" Ian's voice rang off the walls, echoed down the hall.

He started to trot toward the approaching figure. But after a few steps, he stopped with a gasp. The man was wearing the baby-doll mask.

"Dr. Klausmann?" Ian called, his voice high and shrill.

The masked man didn't answer. Just kept walking. Slowly and steadily. Moving toward Ian like some kind of machine. *Or like a puppet,* Ian thought.

"Dr. Klausmann? Have you seen my dad?" Ian cried.

No answer. The man came slowly walking closer. The baby-doll mask glowed pink under the ceiling lights.

Why isn't he answering me? Ian wondered. Fear suddenly tightened his throat and froze him in place.

The man came toward him, hands at his sides. Slow, steady steps, his shoes scraping the marble floor.

Panic kept Ian from turning and running. The grinning baby doll with its red lips was only a few yards away. And then the man stopped inches in front of Ian.

"Dr. Klausmann? Where is my dad? Can you tell me—?"

Silence.

"Please," Ian cried. "Answer me. ANSWER me!"

42

With a desperate cry, Ian raised both hands. He raised both hands—and *ripped* the mask away.

He tore the mask off and stared at the man's face. And then Ian uttered a roaring scream that echoed down the endless hall.

11

"Dad!" Ian cried. "Dad—why didn't you answer me? Why are you wearing the mask?"

His dad's face was red and dripping with sweat from being under the rubber mask. He gazed at Ian a long time. And then his eyes flashed and a grin slowly spread across his face.

"Happy birthday, Ian!" he cried.

The young woman from the office appeared behind them. "Happy birthday, Ian!" she called. She waved to an older man in a black suit. "I'm Linda. And this is Barney. He played the part of Dr. Klausmann."

"Happy birthday," Barney said in his whispery voice.

Mr. Barker slapped Ian on the back. "Gotcha," he said. "That was your birthday adventure, Ian. Did you enjoy it?"

"Enjoy it?" Ian cried. "I—I was terrified!"

"Success!" his dad said. He gave Barney and

Linda a big thumbs-up. "It took a long time to plan this for you."

Ian shook his head. "Wow. I mean, wow. When those dummies all came to life and started to laugh, I totally freaked."

Mr. Barker turned to the two museum workers. "I want to thank you for your time."

"Do I get one of those awesome dummies as a birthday present?" Ian asked.

"No way," his dad answered. "Those dummies are museum pieces, Ian. Maybe someday you can have a dummy of your own. Maybe someday . . ."

As they turned to leave, Ian saw Barney's silvery eyes flash. And in his whispery Dr. Klausmann voice, Barney murmured, "Be careful what you wish for, Ian. Be very careful."

SLAPPY HERE, EVERYONE.

Some people may think Mr. Barker's birthday surprise for Ian was mean. He scared the poor kid half to death.

I thought it was a *scream*. Hahaha!

Did Ian honestly think all those dummies in that museum could come alive?

Whoever heard of such a crazy idea! Hahaha.

Well, it was a birthday Ian never forgot. And he never forgot how much he liked working a ventriloquist dummy and making up jokes with it.

When he got home, he made his own little dummy in art class, with a papier-mâché head and white gloves for hands. He named him Corky and made up a lot of jokes to perform with him.

But the mouth didn't move and neither did the eyes. And the head kept falling off the body. It wasn't the same as a real dummy. And hand puppets just weren't as much fun.

Ian asked his dad to buy him one. Mr. Barker said they were expensive and hard to find. But now, three years later, here we are at Ian's twelfth birthday party. And he's got the real deal—ME! Hahaha.

12

Ian couldn't wait to practice with Slappy. His birthday wish was to become a great ventriloquist. (His other birthday wish was for Jonny and Vinny to go home.)

Now there was the dummy's torn-off hand to deal with.

Mrs. Barker made her way to the kitchen to get lunch ready. Molly disappeared with her doll. The three boys followed Mr. Barker downstairs to his doll hospital to watch him attach Slappy's hand.

Slappy's head thumped hard as Mr. Barker stretched him out on the worktable. "His head weighs a ton," he said. "The puppet maker used very hard wood."

The dolls on the shelves all appeared to stare at them. Their tiny eyes glowed in the bright light from the ceiling.

Vinny picked up two doll legs and made them walk across the table. Jonny found a tall action figure, a doll with a red mask and blue cape. He grabbed it and stabbed his brother in the stomach with it.

"Hey! Watch it!" Vinny grabbed another doll. The two brothers used them as swords, slapping each other in a fast swordfight.

"Hey, guys, that's my work," Mr. Barker said, sighing. "Put them down. Please." He didn't get angry easily. But Ian could see that he was starting to get really annoyed with the two cousins.

Jonny gave his brother one last hard poke in the ribs with the action figure. Then he set it down. Ian watched as his father slid the dummy hand into the jacket sleeve.

"Hey, check this out!" a voice called from the stairs.

Ian turned to see Molly burst into the basement, holding her iPad in front of her. "I looked it up," she said breathlessly. "Do you believe it? Slappy has his own Wikipedia page."

"You're joking," Mr. Barker said. "What does it say?"

Ian stared at his sister. She loved looking things up. She carried her iPad everywhere so she could share information with everyone. She took notes about every doll in her collection. She liked to know all kinds of facts.

"This is so weird," she said. She lowered her eyes to the screen. "It says that Slappy wasn't made by a doll maker or a puppet maker. It says he was built by a sorcerer."

"Huh?" Jonny murmured. "You mean like in Harry Potter?"

"Wikipedia says a sorcerer made him a hundred years ago. And his head was carved out of wood from a coffin. And get this." Molly tapped the screen with her finger. "The coffin was stolen, and it had a curse on it. And so the dummy carries a curse."

Ian squinted at her. "I don't get it. What does that mean?"

"It means you're doomed," Vinny answered. "You're cursed. You're dead meat."

The two brothers giggled and bumped knuckles again.

Ian kept his eyes on Molly. Was she making this up? He didn't think it was funny.

"There's more," Molly said, returning to the screen. "Wikipedia says if you read six magical words out loud, Slappy will come to life."

Ian's mouth dropped open. He suddenly remembered the laughing dummies in the Castle of the Little People. Of course, those dummies hadn't come to life. It was all a trick. But thinking about them gave Ian a chill.

"Magic words! Awesome!" Vinny cried. "What are the words? Let's try it. Read us the words."

Molly bit her bottom lip as she scanned the page. "The words aren't here," she said, shaking her head. "No. No words. They don't have them here."

"Good," Ian said. He felt another chill at the back of his neck. "Maybe it's too dangerous. Maybe they didn't put the words in because the dummy is too dangerous to bring to life."

"You're crazy," Molly told him. "You don't really believe a dummy can come to life—do you?"

Mr. Barker twisted the wooden hand. He pushed it, then pulled it. "It's attached. All fixed," he said. "The hand is on to stay. Just don't have a tug-of-war with it."

He started to sit the dummy up, then stopped as something fell out of the jacket sleeve. "Hey, what's this?" A folded-up slip of paper fell onto the worktable. Mr. Barker reached for it—but Jonny got there first.

Jonny unfolded the paper and squinted at it. "Hey, this has to be it. Six weirdo words. These are the magic words to bring him to life."

"Jonny, don't!" Ian cried. "Don't read them. I'm kind of scared. Please—don't read them! *Please!*"

Jonny chuckled. Then he raised the paper close to his face. And shouted the words one by one:

"Karru Marri Odonna Loma Molonu Karrano!"

13

Ian gasped. A hush fell over the basement. Jonny's words seemed to linger in the air.

All eyes were on the dummy. It lay on its back on the worktable. Its glassy black eyes gazed blankly up at the low ceiling. Its arms hung limply at its sides.

Ian realized he was holding his breath. Was the dummy about to raise his head and speak to them?

Vinny broke the silence. "Maybe you didn't read the words right," he told his brother. "Let me try." He grabbed the paper from Jonny's hand.

But before Vinny could read the first word, Ian took it from him. "I'd better put this in a safe place," he said.

"But it didn't work," Vinny protested. "The dummy didn't move at all."

Mr. Barker smiled. "Not everything on Wikipedia is true," he said.

Ian tucked the paper away in a corner of the worktable. He breathed a sigh of relief. He and some of his friends had watched a horror movie on Netflix about a ventriloquist dummy that came to life and started killing people with an ax. He knew it was just a movie, but he couldn't shake that creepy feeling.

Ian scooped up the dummy and tossed him over his shoulder. "Thanks for fixing him, Dad," he said. He started up the basement stairs to the living room.

The others followed. Molly picked up Abigail and began fiddling with her dress. Jonny and Vinny swiped cupcakes off the tray. They didn't bother to chew, just gulped them down.

Then Vinny made a grab for Slappy. "My turn," he told Ian.

"Not happening," Ian said. "You already broke him once."

They started to argue, but the front door opened and Vinny and Jonny's dad appeared. "Hey, happy birthday, Ian," he called.

"Thanks, Uncle Donny."

Mr. Harding looked a lot like his sons. He was a big, red-faced man, with straight blond hair brushed away from his forehead and striking blue eyes. His face was lined and his expression always reminded Ian of a sad clown he had seen at the circus.

Mr. Harding's stomach bulged under his gray

sweatshirt. His matching gray sweatpants were ripped at one knee.

"Time to go, boys," he told them. "Did you have jackets or anything?"

"No. It's too hot," Vinny answered.

"We don't want to go," Jonny whined. "We didn't get a turn with Slappy. And I'm still hungry."

Mrs. Barker laughed. "Donny, don't you feed these boys? They ate everything but the wallpaper!"

Mr. Harding shook his head. "I'm raising monsters. Seriously."

"You know, next week is the family talent show," Mrs. Barker told Vinny and Jonny. "Maybe you can play with the dummy then."

Vinny groaned. "Another talent show? Do we *have* to?"

"Don't start grumbling," Mr. Harding said. "You know we all get together once a year and have a talent show. It's a wonderful tradition your grandparents started long before you were born."

"It's a dumb tradition," Jonny muttered.

"That's because *you're* dumb," Molly chimed in from the corner of the room.

"Don't start fighting again, Molly," Mrs. Barker snapped. "Your cousins are leaving."

Vinny stomped over to Molly. "What do you want?" she demanded.

54

"Just wanted to say good-bye," Vinny answered. Then he grabbed the head of Molly's doll and snapped it backward.

"You broke it! Dad, he broke it!" Molly shrieked.

Mr. Barker scratched his head. "It looks bad, but I think I can fix it."

Molly glared at Vinny. "Why did you *do* that?"

"Because she's ugly," Vinny said.

"Hey, Vinny—want to talk about ugly?*"* a harsh voice rasped.

Everyone turned to see Slappy moving in Ian's arms.

"Your face looks like something I pulled out of my nose!" Slappy cried.

Vinny growled. "Ian, you jerk. You're not funny!" He rushed at Ian and tried to wrestle the dummy from his arms.

"Guys! Guys!" Uncle Donny pulled Vinny away. "Let's go. Enough fighting." He led Vinny and Jonny to the front door.

"You boys can fight all you want," Molly called after them. "Abigail and I are going to win the talent show next week."

Ian snickered. "Do you honestly think that old doll can compete with Slappy? You're crazy."

"We'll see," Molly said. "We'll see . . ."

14

After dinner the next night, Ian did his homework. Then he picked up Slappy and started to work with the dummy.

He slid his hand around inside the dummy's back, practicing the moves for nodding the head and making the red-lipped mouth go up and down. Ian's hand fumbled around until he found the control for making the dummy's eyes slide back and forth. He practiced moving the eyes until it came naturally for him.

Then Ian practiced talking in a shrill voice without moving his lips. It was harder than he thought. He clamped his teeth together and recited the alphabet. The letter B was impossible to say without touching his lips together. And the letters M and P were just as hard.

Now I need some jokes for our comedy act, Ian thought. But before he could begin, his father's shout rang up the stairs. "Bedtime, Ian. See you at breakfast."

Ian yawned. He wanted to spend more time with Slappy. There were only a few days till the family talent show, and he wanted to be ready. He yawned again. He knew he was too tired to work any longer.

He carried the dummy to his bedroom closet and sat him down against the back wall. Then he pulled out his pajamas and got changed for bed.

Ian fell asleep quickly, with the whisper of a soft breeze outside his open bedroom window. Soon he found himself having the weirdest dream.

Ian dreamed that Vinny and Jonny were ventriloquist dummies. In the dream, they had wooden heads, with their blond hair painted on top. And wooden lips that clicked when their mouths moved up and down.

They were much chubbier than Slappy, and they both had big hands covered by white gloves.

Ian had the Jonny dummy on one lap and the Vinny dummy on the other lap. Somehow, he was able to make them both talk at once. As Ian worked their heads, the two dummies started to shout at one another. Then they began to fight, swinging their arms and smacking each other with their big wooden hands.

Ian lost control. He couldn't stop the fight. The two dummies slid off his lap and began wrestling on the floor, both screaming at once.

Ian woke up laughing. What a crazy dream. His two cousins looked so dumb.

Red morning sunlight washed through the open bedroom window. Ian heard birds chirping in the trees in the front yard.

Blinking himself awake, he started to sit up. "Whoa. Wait."

The closet door was open. Hadn't he closed it tightly last night?

Ian pulled himself all the way up. His arm hit a bump in the covers.

Ian turned. Looked down. And saw the grinning face staring up at him. The grinning face of Slappy, beside him in bed.

15

He's not alive. That's crazy. That's impossible.

Ian shoved the dummy to the edge of the bed. Slappy's eyes gazed blankly into the sunlight from the window. Ian squeezed the dummy's middle. Testing it. Slappy didn't react at all.

No way. He's not alive.

Ian turned and lowered his feet to the floor. A shrill scream from downstairs made him jump up. Was that Molly screaming?

He took off, his bare feet slapping the rug, his heart pounding. He took the stairs two at a time. Another scream rang out. From the kitchen.

He burst through the living room to the dining room to see Molly, red-faced, waving her doll in the air. Their dad stood by the counter, hands on his waist.

"Molly? What's wrong?" Ian demanded.

"Look at her. Just look!" Molly screamed. She waved the doll in Ian's face. "You *know* what's wrong!"

Ian squinted at the doll as Molly jabbed it at him. Abigail's head was turned backward again.

"Ian, how could you do that to your sister?" his dad demanded angrily. "It took me an hour to fix that doll's head. And now you think it's funny to twist it around again?"

"But—but—" Ian sputtered.

"Do you have any idea how valuable the doll is?" Mr. Barker asked.

"How can you be so mean?" Molly wailed. "Were you trying to break Abigail's head off?"

"No way!" Ian cried. "I didn't—"

Mrs. Barker appeared, fastening the belt to her robe. "Ian, we know you want to win the talent contest on Saturday. But you have to play fair."

"But I didn't do it!" Ian screamed. "Read my lips. It wasn't me. I didn't touch Molly's doll."

"Ha!" Molly cried. She brought her face up close to his and shouted it again. "Ha!"

Ian made a disgusted face. "Your breath smells like you ate a dead mouse," he said.

"I don't care!" Molly cried. "Mom and Dad didn't twist the doll's head—*did* they! You're the only other one in the house, Ian. So stop being such a liar."

"Hand me the doll," Mr. Barker said. "I'll take her downstairs and see what I can do. We have to be careful that the head doesn't completely snap off."

Molly handed Abigail to him. Ian saw his mom studying him. *She's looking at me like I'm some kind of criminal,* he thought.

And then he had a brain flash.

He suddenly knew who had twisted Abigail's head around.

16

"YOU did it!" Ian screamed at his sister. "YOU turned the doll's head! I know it!"

Molly spun around, her eyes wide with shock. "Huh? Are you joking?"

"I know you did it," Ian said, jabbing her with his pointer finger.

She danced away from him. "Mom, feel Ian's head. He must have a really high fever. Listen, dumb head, why would I wreck my own doll?"

"To make me look bad," Ian said. "You wanted to make Mom and Dad think that I did it. That I was trying to cheat to win the contest. So you wrecked your own doll."

"Liar!" Molly screamed. "You liar!"

"Stop it—right now." Mrs. Barker stepped between them. "Break it up. Stop being awful to each other. Do you hear me?" She shook her head. "How are we ever going to make it to talent night? And what's the big deal? It's just a family get-together."

"You know Ian," Molly said, sneering. "He has to win everything."

Mrs. Barker pressed her hand over Molly's mouth. "Stop. Truce. Enough, you two. I mean it." She spun Molly around. "I put breakfast on the table. Go eat."

Ian and Molly started toward the breakfast table—but stopped when they saw the grinning figure already sitting there.

"Oh, wow!" Ian cried as the table came into focus. Two glasses had been tipped over, and puddles of orange juice covered the table. The eggs from Molly's plate were smeared over the tablecloth. The seat of Mr. Barker's chair was covered in spilled ketchup.

Slappy sat propped up in Molly's chair, grinning at them, the ketchup bottle in one hand. Ian saw that the dummy had egg smeared on both of his cheeks.

No one said a word. Mom, Dad, and Molly stared hard at Ian.

Ian took a step back. "You—you *can't* think I did this!" he cried in a trembling voice. "You can't. You *can't!*"

17

That Saturday, Ian, Molly, and their two cousins met in Ian's backyard. "There's no way you guys can win," Ian told his cousins. "Because I've had all week to practice with Slappy."

"That's because Ian was grounded all week," Molly added. "He had to stay in his room after dinner every night because of the little joke he played in our kitchen on Monday."

Ian rolled his eyes. "I was grounded for something I didn't do."

Molly shook her head. "Ian, nobody believes you that the dummy messed up the kitchen. Nobody."

The truth was that Ian kept the dummy in the back of his closet all week—because he was terrified of it. Each day, he expected the dummy to stand up and burst out of the closet. Ian was sure that Slappy would do more mischief to cause him trouble.

But to his surprise, the dummy never moved or giggled or talked. It stayed there, folded up in the closet, completely lifeless. Ian began to wonder if maybe the dummy had gone back to sleep for good.

And now, he carried it out for the talent show—mainly because everyone expected it. And because Ian had no other talent he could present.

"We're not too worried about you and your dummy," Jonny told Ian. He waved a big wooden duckpin in Ian's face. "Vinny and I have been practicing, too. And we're awesome."

"We're going to start our own YouTube channel," Vinny said. "And we're going to have millions of subscribers."

Ian laughed. "Why would anyone watch a juggling channel on YouTube? Get serious. Why would anyone spend more than five seconds watching you toss short, fat bowling pins back and forth?"

"Because we're awesome," Jonny said. He flipped the heavy duckpin in the air, high over his head, and caught it behind his back. "You should just give up. Vinny and I have this locked."

The four kids were standing in the shade of a wide maple tree in the Barkers' backyard. The warm Saturday afternoon sunlight felt more like summer than spring. The sun made all the fresh leaves sparkle like beaded jewels on the trees.

Jonny and Vinny needed a lot of space for their duckpin juggling. So Mr. and Mrs. Barker decided their act would be better outdoors. They set up chairs facing the flat grassy area in the center of the yard. Then they disappeared into the house.

"Hey, what's keeping you guys?" Vinny shouted into the kitchen window. His mother wasn't feeling well, so Mr. Harding came alone. "It's showtime!"

Mr. and Mrs. Barker and Mr. Harding finally came out of the house, carrying glasses of iced tea. All three of them were talking at once. Ian couldn't really hear what it was about. Something about politics, he thought.

Jonny flipped a duckpin high over his head again. It came down end-over-end, and this time he missed it. It bounced heavily on the ground with a loud *thud*.

Mr. Barker shielded his eyes from the sun with one hand. "You guys are juggling duckpins now?" he said. "What happened to your juggling act with the white dinner plates?"

"They broke too many of them," Mr. Harding said. "The duckpins should last longer."

The three adults sat down on folding chairs. Molly, holding Abigail in her lap, sat cross-legged in the grass. Ian stood at her side, holding Slappy against his chest.

"We're first," Vinny said. He had four duckpins clamped in his hands. He carried them to the center of the yard.

"We're first and we're best," Jonny said.

"*We'll* be the judge of that," his dad said.

"Uncle Donny should have *two* votes, since Aunt Marie isn't here," Molly said.

"Yes. Sweet!" Vinny declared. "And you'll vote for us—right, Dad?"

"I'll vote for the best act," Mr. Harding said. "Are you two going to talk our heads off, or are you going to juggle?"

Ian reached down and squeezed Molly's shoulder. "Better not sit too close. They'll probably bean you."

Jonny turned and shook his head. "No way. You're about to witness total control."

They took their places several yards apart. Vinny pulled down the visor of his baseball cap to keep the bright sun from his eyes. They faced each other, standing straight, shoulders back.

Vinny set three of the four duckpins on the grass beside him. He raised the remaining pin in his right hand. "We start with one pin," he announced. "We end up with *four* pins in the air at once!"

Jonny leaned forward and reached out a hand. Vinny sent the duckpin flying end over end. Its shadow shot across the grass. Jonny caught it easily and, in one motion, sent it sailing back to his brother.

A few seconds later, there were two pins flying back and forth. And then three. The boys kept their arms whirling. The pins flew rapidly. They caught them in rhythm and sent them toppling back.

The three adults began to clap. Molly clapped, too. Ian hugged Slappy to his chest. Ian's eyes darted left, then right, following the pins.

"Great job!" Mr. Barker shouted. "You boys look like pros."

The two boys kept their eyes straight ahead. Their hands worked fast. Like machines. The pins flew faster and faster between them.

They're really good, Ian thought.

Then they heard a hard *thud* that made Ian and Molly jump.

Ian wasn't sure he was seeing right. Did a duckpin just smash into Jonny's head and bounce to the ground?

Mrs. Barker screamed. Both dads leapt to their feet, openmouthed.

Jonny's eyes bulged. A soft moan escaped his throat. His knees folded and he went down on the grass. Crumpled, his body folded up on itself. He didn't move.

"It was an accident!" Vinny screamed, running to his brother. "The pin slipped. It was an accident."

"Oh no. Oh no. Oh no." Mrs. Barker had her hands pressed to her cheeks.

Mr. Harding was down on one knee, leaning

over his son. "Jonny, can you hear me? Jonny? Can you open your eyes?"

"We may need a doctor," Mr. Barker said. "He's out. He's unconscious."

Holding Slappy tightly around his middle, Ian gasped when the dummy suddenly began to move. As the adults huddled over the fallen boy, Slappy tossed his head back—and let out a long, ringing, gleeful laugh.

18

The dummy's cold laughter rang out over the yard.

"Ian—what's *wrong* with you?" Mr. Barker shouted, looking up from the folded body of Jonny at his feet. "That's not funny. Your cousin is really hurt."

Molly turned to scold him. "Make Slappy stop! That's horrible, Ian. Make him stop!"

"I . . . I can't!" Ian cried. His voice cracked. His throat tightened in fear. "I'm not doing it! I swear." He shook the dummy hard in both hands. Finally, the wooden mouth snapped shut and the cruel laughter stopped.

Mr. Barker shook a finger at Ian. "You and I are going to have a serious talk later," he said.

"But, Dad—" Ian started. "I swear . . ."

Molly frowned at Ian. "What's your problem? That was totally dumb."

Ian didn't answer. Frightening thoughts shot through his mind. The dummy was definitely acting on his own. How could Ian make anyone believe him? He took a few steps toward Jonny.

Vinny paced back and forth across the lawn. He still held a duckpin in each hand. He turned to Ian. "It just slipped," he said. "I didn't mean to throw it that hard."

"Everyone knows it was an accident," Ian told him.

Down on the grass, Jonny groaned. He opened his eyes. He blinked them several times. "Did I get hit?" he asked, rubbing his forehead.

His dad nodded. "You're going to have a very big bump on your head."

"I think I have a headache," Jonny said, blinking his eyes some more.

"My hand slipped," Vinny told him. "I didn't mean to—"

Jonny waved a hand. "It wasn't your fault. I should have kept my head out of the way."

That made everyone laugh. Mr. Harding helped Jonny sit up. "Are you dizzy? Do you feel light-headed?"

"Of course he feels light-headed," Slappy suddenly chimed in. *"There's no brain in there!"*

Everyone turned to Ian. "Put the dummy down," Mr. Barker said. "Do you really think this is a time for jokes?"

"I . . . uh . . ." Ian stammered. "I'm just happy that Jonny is okay."

The two men each took an arm and pulled Jonny to his feet. "Do you feel strange? Can you stand up?"

Jonny nodded. "I feel pretty good. I just have a headache. You know. It's kind of throbbing right here." He tenderly rubbed his right temple. He turned to Mr. Barker. "Does this mean that Vinny and I don't win?"

"You can still win," Ian's dad told him. "You guys were terrific . . . for a while."

"We'll have to see the other talents before we decide," Mrs. Barker said.

They made Jonny walk back and forth across the back lawn. "I feel okay," he said. "I'm not dizzy or anything."

"We need to put ice on that bump," Mrs. Barker said. She took him by the shoulder. "Come on, everyone. Let's go inside."

Ian tossed Slappy over his shoulder and followed the others into the house. *This day isn't going well at all*, he thought. *First, Jonny gets clonked in the head and knocked out. Then Slappy starts laughing and making jokes without me.*

Ian was desperate to talk about it with his parents. He was desperate to tell them he wasn't always in control of Slappy.

But everyone was clustered around Jonny. They planted him in the big, comfy armchair in the living room, made him put his feet up on an ottoman, and gave him a blue ice pack to press against his forehead.

Molly set Abigail down on the dining room table and disappeared upstairs. Ian set Slappy down beside Molly's doll. Mr. Barker walked into the kitchen and came out a few minutes later with big bowls of tortilla chips and cans of Coke. Vinny had found Ian's phone and was standing in a corner, playing a game on it.

After a while, Jonny set the ice pack down at his side. "I feel okay. Really," he said. "I think we should finish the talent show."

"Are you sure you feel all right?" Mrs. Barker asked.

Jonny convinced everyone that he was fine, so Mrs. Barker called Molly down from upstairs. "You're next, Molly. What is your talent going to be?"

"I'm going to do a fashion show with Abigail," she answered. "With dresses that I designed and made. Get ready to be impressed."

"Everyone take a seat," Mrs. Barker said. "Vinny, put down that game and join the rest of us. Let's check out these outfits that Molly made for her doll."

"Hey, wait!" Molly screamed. "Where's Abigail?"

Ian turned and caught the distressed look on his sister's face.

"Where is Abigail?" Molly demanded. "I set her down on the table and—"

Her eyes suddenly went wide. Her mouth dropped open. And she let out a horrified scream: "Oh noooo! I don't believe it!"

19

Ian turned and saw what his sister was screaming about. He uttered a sharp cry as his eyes focused on Abigail, floating on her side, near the bottom of their goldfish tank.

No one moved. It was as if they were paralyzed by shock.

Then Molly let out another shrill scream—and leaped at Ian. "How could you? How *could* you?" she wailed. She pounded his chest with both fists. "Ian, you creep! How could you drown Abigail?"

"No! No way! Not me!" Ian screamed.

But Molly was too furious to hear him. She shoved him backward, punching his chest with all her strength. "You creep! You creep! You ruined my doll!"

Ian tried to tell her he didn't do it. But the words caught in his throat. Molly shoved him again, and he lost his balance. He stumbled and fell backward—smashing against the fish tank.

"Oh nooo." He felt it slide off the table. Before he could catch his balance, he heard the crash of the tank on the floor, the shatter of glass.

All three adults were shouting now. Molly, red-faced, had tears rolling down both cheeks. The drenched doll rolled out from the broken fish tank and lay facedown in a puddle of water and jagged shards of glass. The three goldfish jerked and flopped on the floor, gasping their last breaths.

Ian spun away from the table, his heart pounding. He lifted the doll off the floor and handed it to Molly. With a roar of fury, she swung it hard, aiming at his face.

"Wait! Wait!" he cried, dancing away from her. "You're wrong, Molly! It wasn't me!"

Mrs. Barker knelt over the broken fish tank. "Step back, everybody. Don't cut yourselves on the glass." Ian's dad picked up the three fish and, holding them between his hands, rushed to the kitchen to find some water for them to swim in.

Vinny and Jonny stood with their dad across the room. All three of them stared at Ian.

"You've *got* to listen to me!" Ian cried. "I didn't do it!"

"Abigail didn't *jump* in!" Molly shouted, holding the wet doll to her chest. "You're such a liar, Ian. Who *else* would do it?"

Ian's mom was carefully lifting shards of glass off the floor and dropping them in her palm. "I'm very disappointed in you, Ian," she said. "Why were you so desperate to win? It's just a family contest."

Ian balled his hands into tight fists. "Isn't anyone going to listen to me?" he said through gritted teeth. "I didn't put the doll in the fish tank. I *swear* I didn't." He pointed at his cousins across the room. "Why don't you ask *them* who did it?"

Vinny and Jonny both started talking at once.

"I was sitting in the living room with the ice pack on my head," Jonny said. "You saw me. I didn't move."

"Don't try to blame me," Vinny said. "I was across from my brother the whole time."

Mr. Barker returned, carrying the three goldfish in a big glass measuring cup filled with water. "Do you swear you didn't do it, Ian?" he asked.

Ian raised his right hand. "I swear."

"Dad, he's lying," Molly insisted. "Look at my doll. She's ruined forever."

"I think I can dry her out," her dad replied. "I can probably get Abigail looking good again."

"Do you believe me, Dad?" Ian asked.

Mr. Barker frowned. "I don't know *what* to believe."

"The talent show is a disaster," Uncle Donny said. He turned Jonny's face toward him to examine the bump on his forehead. It was still bright red. "I think we should go home and nurse our wounds."

"Wait," Ian's mom said. "I think we should let Ian do his act."

"Huh?" Ian's mouth dropped open. "Are you sure?" Ian had a heavy feeling in the pit of his stomach. He had a bad feeling about this.

"Go ahead," Mrs. Barker urged. "I'll bet it's funny. You've been practicing all week. Go ahead, Ian. It will cheer us all up."

Ian shrugged. "I'm not sure . . ."

"Ian should save his act for another time," Uncle Donny said.

"It's still early. Why not let him do it?" Mrs. Barker said. "End the day on a happy note."

"I'd like to see what he's worked up," Mr. Barker said.

While everyone was still talking, Vinny strode over to the dining room table. "Hey, why don't I get a turn with the dummy?" he asked. "I can be funny, too."

Vinny lifted Slappy off the table and started to push his hand into the opening in the dummy's back. But he stopped, and his face filled with surprise.

"Whoa," he said. "Look. The dummy's hands are wet."

Ian dove across the room and yanked Slappy from Vinny's arms. "Oh, wow," he murmured. "The hands *are* wet."

"That's not going to fool anyone," Molly said, crossing her arms in front of her. "So you dipped Slappy's hands in the fish tank. Big whoop. Are we really supposed to think that Slappy shoved my doll under the water?"

Ian stared at her. He didn't know how to answer. Molly wouldn't believe him, no matter what he said. And he knew he was telling the truth. He never touched her doll. And he never moved Slappy from the table.

He studied Slappy's face. Was the dummy's grin a little wider than before? No. No way. Ian had to be imagining that.

"Ian, sit down and do your ventriloquist act for us," his dad said.

"Yes. Let's get this evening over with," Uncle Donny said, rolling his eyes.

"Give Ian a chance," Mrs. Barker scolded him. "We don't want to be unfair to him."

Suddenly, Slappy spoke up: *"Someone was unfair to you, Mrs. Barker. Why did they give you a face that could break mirrors?"*

Ian's mom shook her head. "Not funny, Ian. I hope you practiced better jokes than that."

Ian felt a chill at the back of his neck. *I didn't say that awful joke. The dummy is speaking without me.*

He didn't want to continue. This was *terrifying.* But he was trapped. They were all watching him eagerly, even Vinny and Jonny.

Ian sat down sideways on a dining room chair and propped the dummy on his lap. Uncle Donny squeezed between Ian's two cousins on the couch. Ian's parents shared the big armchair beside the couch. Molly remained standing with her arms tightly crossed, an angry expression locked on her face.

Ian stuck his hand in the dummy's back and made the wooden lips click up and down. *"Did you make the dinner tonight, Mrs. Barker?"* Slappy asked. *"I'm sorry, but I throw up better food than that."*

"Ian—please," his mother said. "Not so rude. You can be funny without being rude."

"But—" Ian tried to explain, but Slappy cut him off.

"You want to see funny? Look in a mirror!" Slappy rasped.

The dummy turned to Molly. *"Good news, Molly,"* Slappy said. *"They're looking for someone to play a pig on Animal Planet. You don't even have to audition. You've got the part!"*

Molly let out a disgusted groan. "Make Ian stop, Mom."

"Molly, here's a riddle. What's the difference between you and a dead, rotting bird on the sidewalk?"

Molly rolled her eyes. "I don't know."

"Hahahaha. I don't know, either!"

"Ian, your jokes aren't nice," his mom said.

"You know what's nice?" Slappy demanded. *"When you leave a room, and it starts to smell better!"*

Mrs. Barker jumped to her feet. "Ian—I'm warning you!"

"I . . . I didn't say it," Ian stammered. "Slappy said it. I—I—"

"Uncle Donny, is that really your face? Or did someone barf all over your shoulders?" the dummy rasped.

Mr. Barker stood up and shook a finger at Ian. "Enough barf jokes," he said. "I mean it. If you can't do nicer jokes—"

"Mr. Barker," the dummy interrupted. *"I don't*

want to say you stink. But you give diarrhea *a bad name! Hahahaha!"*

"That's enough. You're finished!" Mr. Barker cried. "Go to your room, Ian."

"Hey, Molly—know how to make yourself prettier? Stick your head in a Cuisinart and push START.*"*

"Go to your room, Ian," Mr. Barker repeated, "and take the dummy with you."

"Jonny and Vinny—you two guys look exactly like something I stepped in at the dog park!"

Mr. Barker took Ian firmly by the shoulder and guided him to the stairs. "Go. You're in a lot of trouble, young man. We're going to have a long talk about this."

"You . . . you have to believe me, Dad," Ian stammered. "Those aren't my jokes. I . . . I didn't say those things. Really. I—"

"Ian, just go." His dad gave him a push up the stairs.

"Why won't anyone listen to me?" Ian screamed. "The dummy is alive! The dummy is saying those horrible jokes!"

"Just go," Mr. Barker said, his cheeks reddening with anger. "I'm not going to say it again."

Ian sighed. With the dummy slung over his shoulder, he turned and began to trudge slowly up the stairs. To his horror, Slappy opened his mouth wide and giggled all the way up.

21

Ian slumped into his room and slammed the door shut behind him. "Shut up! Shut up! Shut up!" he cried. But Slappy wouldn't stop giggling.

Ian grabbed the dummy by its shoulders and shook it, shook it hard, making its wooden head bounce. "Shut up! Shut up!"

Slappy's eyes twirled and he giggled louder.

With a cry of disgust, Ian pulled open his closet door and heaved the dummy to the back of the closet. Slappy bounced off the wall and folded over himself, sprawled in a pile of dirty T-shirts and jeans. He finally stopped his annoying laughter.

Ian gripped the closet door handle tightly and stared at the dummy for a long moment. "Are you going to sit up now? Are you going to talk to me? Are you going to get me in more trouble? WHY ARE YOU DOING THIS TO ME?"

Ian realized he was trembling, his whole body shaking in fear. The dummy was alive and he

83

was the only one who knew it. No one believed him. No one. He was alone here with this . . . this *creature.*

The dummy didn't move. Not a twitch. It remained folded over itself on the closet floor.

Ian shut the closet. He made sure it clicked securely. *I wish I had a lock on this door.*

He began to pace back and forth across his room. He held his hands tightly clasped in front of him. He couldn't stop trembling, couldn't stop the shudders that rolled down his back.

Those words . . . Those weird words must have brought him to life.

But what did the dummy want? Just to embarrass him in front of his family? To get him in trouble?

"I should have known something was wrong with this dummy just from the evil grin on its painted mouth," Ian told himself. "Dad should have known better. Someone sent Dad the dummy with no return address. Of *course* they didn't put a return address. They didn't want it back."

Ian shuddered again. He didn't want the dummy, either.

But how could he get rid of it? He was going to need help. So first, he had to convince everyone that he was telling the truth. He had to prove to them that the dummy was alive.

He suddenly felt weary. Worn out. He glanced at the clock above his desk. Half an hour past his bedtime. Could he sleep? Could he sleep knowing that the dummy was alive inside the closet?

He took a deep breath and pulled open the closet door. He expected Slappy to be standing there, ready to jump out at him. But no. The dummy hadn't moved. It sat in a lifeless heap with its head bowed.

Ian let out a long sigh. Once again, he carefully closed the door, making sure it clicked tightly. Should he put a chair or something heavy to block it? Ian yawned. He was suddenly too sleepy to think about it.

He pulled off his clothes and tossed them on the floor. Then he found a pair of pajamas in his dresser drawer and tugged them on.

A warm breeze ruffled the curtains at his bedroom window. He heard a car honk somewhere in the distance. He climbed into bed and pulled the covers up to his chin.

Ian fell asleep as soon as his head hit the pillow.

How long did he sleep? Not very long. He was awakened by a thump and a scraping sound.

"Huh?" Ian sat straight up, blinking himself awake. He realized it wasn't morning. He could see a sliver of a moon in the night sky.

He heard another thump. A bump. Someone walking around? Walking in the dark?

His senses were all alert now. His skin tingled. He struggled to focus in the dim light.

Another footstep.

He started to stand up. His feet tangled in the bedsheet. He nearly fell.

"Hey!" He caught his balance and stepped away from the bed. He gazed around the room. "Whoa." Ian saw right away what had changed.

The closet door was open.

A chill rolled slowly down his back. He forced himself to walk to the closet. He grabbed the door and clicked on the light. He peered to the back of the closet.

Slappy was gone.

22

Ian felt his knees start to fold. He gripped the edge of the closet door to keep himself up. He squinted into the closet. Yellow light from the ceiling bulb spread over the closet floor. The empty closet floor.

Ian kept thinking maybe he was still asleep. Maybe he was dreaming this. Maybe he was sleepwalking and dreaming that the dummy had picked himself up and walked away.

But he knew he was awake. And another soft *thud* from the hallway, another footstep heading toward the stairs, snapped him completely alert. And he suddenly knew this was his chance.

Slappy was walking to the stairs. And this was Ian's chance to get the proof he needed. The proof he needed to show his parents that Slappy was *alive*.

"My phone," he murmured. "Where did I leave my phone?"

He gazed around the room. Not on his desk, where he usually left it. Not plugged into the charger near his bed. Ian saw his jeans piled in the center of the floor. He picked them up and fumbled through the pockets.

"Yes!"

He grabbed the phone in his trembling hand and pushed the camera icon.

Ready.

Ian stepped into the hall. A dim night-light at the floor cast a pale cone of light over one wall. No one there.

Slappy must be making his way down the stairs.

Holding his breath, Ian tiptoed over the soft carpet, hurrying to the stairway. He raised the phone in front of him, ready to capture his proof. A photo of the dummy walking down the steps by himself would *have* to convince his parents that he was telling the truth.

He heard another soft *thud*. The stairs creaked.

Ignoring the chills that swept down his back, Ian stepped to the top of the stairs. Darkness below, but he could see the dummy moving slowly down, one step at a time, a hand sliding along the banister.

Yes. Got him.

Ian raised the camera, aimed it down the stairs—and clicked a photo.

He blinked in the lightning-white burst of the flash.

Click. He flashed another one. Another burst of white light.

And Ian opened his mouth in a startled gasp. "Oh no! No way!"

23

The hall light flashed on. Ian lowered his phone and squinted down the stairs at his dad.

Not Slappy. His dad. In his maroon bathrobe. His hair wild about his head from sleep. Halfway down the stairs.

"D-dad," Ian stammered, "I thought—"

Mr. Barker turned. "Ian? Were you walking around? I thought I heard someone walking around upstairs. I came to investigate."

"I heard something, too," Ian said. "It woke me up. I thought it was footsteps and—"

"What on earth!" Mr. Barker cried. He pointed. "Look. The front door is wide open."

Ian's heart began to pound in his chest. He grabbed the banister, squeezing it tightly in his clammy hand. "It—it's Slappy," he said.

Mr. Barker frowned. "This isn't a good time for your Slappy stories," he said. He turned and hurried down the remaining stairs and crossed the hall to the front door.

"Dad, listen to me." Ian followed him. He stepped up beside him and gazed out the open door. The sliver of a moon hung low in a purple sky. Ian saw Molly's scooter on its side beside the driveway. A rabbit stood frozen on its hind legs near the curb, its ears straight up, black eyes glowing.

No one else out there.

"It's Slappy, Dad. You have to believe me. I heard him leave my room."

Mr. Barker put a hand on Ian's shoulder. "You *what*?"

"It woke me up. I heard him walking out in the hallway. He isn't there, Dad. I closed him in my closet. I made sure the door was shut. But he's gone."

Mr. Barker pushed the front door closed and turned the lock. "The dummy isn't in your closet?"

Ian shook his head. "No. He's gone."

Ian's dad scratched his head. "There's got to be an explanation."

"Yes, there is, Dad," Ian said. "Slappy is *alive*. He's alive and he's dangerous. And he's out prowling the neighborhood on his own."

SLAPPY HERE, GUYS.

Smart kid, that Ian. He spoke the truth.

Slappy is alive and he's dangerous.

I couldn't describe myself any better if I tried. Hahaha.

It's about time Mr. Barker caught on, don't you agree? He's not exactly the brightest crayon in the box. I don't want to say he is dumb—but tell me why his IQ is the same number as his *belt size*? Hahahaha.

Of course, what do you expect? The man spends all his time playing with dolls!

He didn't pay much attention to me when I was in his doll hospital. I don't think he appreciated how *cute* I am. I'm better than cute. You might even say I'm a *living doll*! Hahahaha.

Well, I hope you're enjoying this story as much as I am. I like a story where the humans are totally confused about what's going on. Who's the dummy in this story? It ain't me, dudes!

Let's change the scene now. We'll leave Ian and his dad scratching their heads at the front door. And let's move a few blocks away.

Yes, that little brick house is where Jonny and Vinny live. Why don't we see what those two lovable rascals are up to? It might actually surprise *even you*! Hahahaha!

24

Vinny slapped his brother on the back. "Way to go, Jonny!"

Jonny slapped him back. "Way to go, Vinny!"

The two boys bumped knuckles. They slapped high fives. They did a hard chest bump that left them both breathless. Then they did a crazy dance all around their bedroom, laughing and giggling.

A major celebration.

Slappy stared at them blankly from where they had propped him up on Vinny's bed. The dummy sat lifelessly, arms hanging limply down at his sides.

The boys shared a room in the back of their house. There was only enough space for two twin beds and a small dresser. The boys shared a laptop computer that sat on a card table against one wall.

Vinny picked up Slappy and raised him till they were face-to-face. "Welcome to our house, dummy," he said. "Guess what? You've been kidnapped!"

That made both boys howl with laughter. They bumped knuckles again. Then they raised Slappy's wooden hand and bumped knuckles with him.

"Ian won't have a clue," Jonny said.

Vinny chuckled. "He's such a dweebo. He'll probably think the dummy walked out on his own!"

He lowered Slappy until the dummy's brown leather shoes touched the floor. "Go ahead, dummy. Let's see you walk."

He moved the dummy along the floor. "Come on. Aren't you going to walk for us, Slappy?"

"Ian believed that lame story about magic words that bring the dummy to life," Jonny said, shaking his head. "The guy probably believes in the Easter Bunny, too."

"Whatever you do," Vinny said, "don't tell him there's no Tooth Fairy. You'll break his little heart. He'll freak out."

That made the boys laugh some more.

"Hey, what's all the racket?" Their father's voice came from the bedroom next to theirs.

"Nothing," Jonny shouted back.

"It's very late." Mr. Harding groaned. "What are you doing?"

"Nothing."

"Just kidnapping a dummy," Vinny whispered, grinning at his brother.

"Well, I'm going to sleep. So be quiet in there," their father called. "Tomorrow is Sunday. You can mess around all day. But let your mother and me get some sleep."

"No problem," Vinny shouted through the wall. He sat Slappy down on the floor. "Ian will probably be looking for him all night," he said, shaking his head. "He'll have his whole family out searching for a *living* dummy."

"Leaving their front door open was brilliant," Jonny said.

"It was *your* idea," Vinny told him.

Jonny grinned. "I know. That's why it was brilliant."

"Ian will be totally confused. His brain will explode."

"What a dummy," Jonny said.

They both hee-hawed at that.

They fell asleep still giggling over the wonderful crime they had committed. They woke up a little after nine the next morning. Vinny grinned when he saw Slappy on the floor beside his bed.

"I thought maybe I dreamed that we kidnapped him," he said.

"No. We really did it," Jonny replied, still yawning from sleep.

Vinny lifted Slappy onto his lap and slipped a hand into his back. He made the dummy's mouth slide up and down. *"Hello, boys and ghouls,"* he made Slappy say in a tinny voice. *I'm a dummy. How about you?"*

"You're moving your lips," Jonny said. "You're not doing it right. Here. Give him to me."

Jonny lifted Slappy off his brother's lap. He shoved his hand into the dummy's back. He made the eyes dart from side to side. "I found the eye controls. Cool," Jonny said.

He made the mouth work, the wooden lips clicking together. *"Vinny rhymes with skinny,"* he made the dummy say. *"Vinny isn't skinny. He's about as skinny as a cow."*

"Not funny," Vinny said, tugging Slappy away from his brother. "Not funny—and you moved your lips."

"Give me a chance," Jonny said. He grabbed the dummy's hand and tried to pull it back. "I need to practice."

"You need to let go," Vinny said. He shook a fist at his brother and Jonny lifted his hand from the dummy.

"What do you think Ian is doing right now?" Vinny said.

"Probably hiding under his bed. Terrified the living dummy will come back to get him."

They both laughed. Vinny set the dummy down on his bed.

"We should send him a ransom note," Vinny said.

"A ransom note?"

"You know. Make him pay to get his precious dummy back," Vinny said. "How much should we ask for?"

"A million dollars?" Jonny replied.

Vinny laughed. "No. That's not enough. How about five million?"

They started to laugh again. But they both stopped short when Slappy raised his head. The dummy's eyes slid back and forth, then stopped on the two startled boys.

"Had your fun, punks?" Slappy rasped. *"Now it's MY turn. Are you ready to enter a world of PAIN?"*

25

Jonny made a choking sound. Vinny's eyes nearly bulged out of his head.

"Did you make him say that?" Jonny cried.

Vinny shook his head. "No. No way." His eyes were still wide with fright. His mouth hung open. Both boys stared at the dummy.

Slappy's eyes slid back and forth. He giggled. Suddenly, one of his big wooden hands swung up hard—and *smacked* Vinny in the nose.

Vinny cried out and staggered back, blinking in pain. He grabbed his nose. "Hey—you gave me a nosebleed!"

"I've got one, too!" the dummy screeched. *"Look!"*

Slappy tilted his head back—and a thick stream of bright green goo came shooting from his nostrils. The dummy turned his head and shot a powerful wave of goo over Vinny.

Vinny tried to squirm away. Too late. The thick, lumpy liquid splashed over his head, down his face, and down the front of his shirt. "It's *hot*!" Vinny shrieked. "Owwww. It's boiling hot."

Slappy giggled again and, keeping his head tilted back, kept spraying disgusting goo on Vinny.

"It stinks!" Vinny wailed, thrashing his arms as the liquid poured over him, dropping to his knees. "And it's burning me! Help! It's burning me! Don't just stand there. Help me!"

Jonny's mouth was frozen open, his face pale with horror. He took a deep breath, then dove at the dummy. Slappy ducked to the side. Jonny missed him and landed facedown on the bed.

Before he could move, Slappy swung a hand and clonked Jonny on the head.

Jonny screamed. The dummy had hit the bump still sore from the duckpin. Jonny grabbed his forehead as stab after stab of pain nearly blinded him.

Before Jonny could move, Slappy turned his head—and sent a gob of the disgusting green goo from his nose plopping over Jonny.

Jonny spun on the bed and slipped to the floor. Slappy splashed the green goo onto Jonny's back, over the back of his head. Jonny howled in pain.

"Mom! Dad!" Vinny screamed, slapping at the green gunk that covered him. "Help us! Can you hear us?"

"Once they're asleep, it's impossible to wake them up," his brother moaned.

"Please—wake up! Wake up! We need help!" Vinny cried.

Slappy tossed back his head and cackled. *"Welcome to SlappyWorld, boys!"*

26

Vinny struggled to back away. On the floor, the hot puddle of goo bubbled over his bare ankles. He tugged the sheet off his bed and used it as a towel, wiping the putrid gunk off his face, his hair, his shoulders.

Jonny climbed off the bed, mopping his face with both hands. The hot gunk burned his skin. The sour odor made his stomach churn.

Slappy had stopped spewing from his nostrils. Now he sat against the headboard, a grin on his painted red lips, his eyes darting from side to side.

"This is impossible!" Vinny cried, wiping goo from his hair. "It's just impossible!"

"Know what's impossible?" Slappy rasped. *"That someone with such a fat head should have such a tiny brain! Do you hear it rattling around in your skull?"*

Jonny made another choking sound. "He's really talking all by himself," he said to his brother. "He . . . he's alive."

"*You guys aren't exactly brilliant,*" the dummy shouted. "*The only thing your heads are good for is to keep your hats off your shoulders! Hahahaha! I know you failed your IQ tests because you couldn't spell IQ!*"

"This . . . is impossible," Vinny repeated. "A dummy can't talk on his own."

"*Then what's YOUR excuse?*" Slappy cried. He laughed his shrill, cold laugh.

Jonny turned to his brother. "We never should have kidnapped him."

Slappy snickered. "*You guys may not be smart. But at least you're ugly.*"

Vinny groaned. He took a few steps toward the bed, his eyes locked on Slappy's grinning face. He remembered not to get too close. His nose still throbbed from the dummy's wooden punch.

"What do you want?" Vinny demanded. "Stop the jokes."

"*You two are the jokes!*" Slappy replied.

"Just tell us what you want!" Vinny cried.

"*I want to tell you your new names,*" the dummy replied.

Jonny and Vinny exchanged glances. "New names? What new names?" Vinny demanded.

"*Your new names are Slave One and Slave Two.*"

"Are you joking?" Jonny said.

The dummy leaned forward. "*Are you breathing? It's hard to tell if a slug is breathing.*"

"You mean you think we'll be your slaves?" Vinny asked.

"*Let's stop wasting time,*" Slappy replied. "*You ARE my slaves. If you do a good job, maybe I'll give you Christmas off. Hahahaha!*"

"You're crazy!" Jonny cried. "You can't control us!"

Slappy ignored Jonny's words. "*Here's your first assignment,*" he said. "*I want you to go back to Ian's house.*"

"Can we take you there?" Vinny asked. "Can we take you back there? It's where you belong."

"*You belong where you were born,*" Slappy snapped. "*Under a rock.*"

"We'll take you back right away," Vinny said.

"*Right away isn't soon enough!*" Slappy screamed. "*Now shut up and listen to your master's assignment for you. You will take me back to Ian's, and you will help me find the slip of paper.*"

"What slip of paper?" Jonny demanded.

"*The paper that has the secret words on it, dummy,*" Slappy snapped. "*I don't want anyone ever saying those words again. If someone reads the words again, I'll go back to sleep. I can't allow that. I'm alive! ALIVE! Get it, you dead heads?! Hahahaha.*"

Jonny and Vinny exchanged glances. "Is this really happening?" Vinny murmured.

"And don't get any funny ideas about reading the words yourselves," Slappy rasped. *"I can have another scalding-hot nosebleed on you guys. Don't forget. Now let's get going."*

Vinny motioned toward the bedroom door with his eyes. Jonny quickly caught on.

"Uh . . . I don't think so," Vinny said softly. "I don't think that's going to happen."

"And you know what?" Jonny chimed in. "That whole slave thing? That's not going to happen, either."

Before Slappy could reply, Vinny burst forward and gave the dummy a hard shove with both hands. The shove sent Slappy toppling to the floor. His wooden head made a loud *clonk* as it bounced off the floorboards.

Vinny and Jonny took off to the bedroom door. Jonny got there first. He wrapped his hand around the knob, twisted it, and pulled.

"Hey!" Both boys uttered cries.

Jonny tried the door again. It wouldn't budge.

They turned back to Slappy, who had climbed to his feet, eyes wide, hands on the top of the bed.

"The door . . . it's locked," Vinny stammered.

Slappy snickered. *"Do you think I'm a dummy? Of COURSE it's locked. Maybe we should change your names. How about Prisoner One and Prisoner Two?"*

He took a few steps toward them. He walked

in a jerky motion. His legs were light and rubbery. His heavy shoes scraped the floor.

Jonny spun away from the dummy and tried the door one more time. Vinny watched the dummy approach. His eyes were wide with disbelief. "If we find you the sheet of paper, will you leave us alone?"

"Of course not," Slappy said. *"You are both mine now. What is it about being a slave that you don't understand?"*

Both boys jumped when they heard a hard knock on the other side of the bedroom door. "Hey—what's going on in there?" their mom shouted from the hallway.

"Mom! Help us!" Jonny cried.

Vinny pushed Jonny out of the way and grabbed the door handle. He twisted the knob and gave a hard tug, so hard it made him groan.

The door swung open.

Mrs. Harding stood there, a startled look on her face.

"Mom—help us!" Vinny cried. "The dummy— it's alive. It's alive!"

27

Mrs. Harding swept past the two boys in the doorway and burst into the room. "What on earth are you talking about?"

She was short and very thin and wore a long white sweatshirt over maroon sweatpants. She had been sick for a while and her now-baggy clothes hung loosely on her. Her blond hair had streaks of gray in it, which the boys hadn't noticed before.

She squinted from Jonny to Vinny. "Slappy? Here? What are you so worked up about?"

She gazed down and saw the dummy, folded up in a heap, facedown on the floor beside the bed.

"He—he's alive!" Vinny stammered, pointing down at the dummy with a trembling finger. "He's crazy, Mom!"

Mrs. Harding walked over to the dummy. "Are you sure *he's* the one that's crazy?" she said. "It's just a dummy, guys." She poked it gently with the toe of her sneaker.

Slappy's chest hit the floor. He lay limply, arms beneath him, eyes shut tight.

She turned back to Jonny and Vinny. "Are you playing some kind of joke? You don't really expect me to think that this dummy is alive—do you? Have you two been seeing too many horror movies? I'll take away your Netflix. I mean it."

"Mom, please—" Jonny begged.

"What's it doing here?" she demanded. "Did Ian loan it to you?"

"Never mind," Vinny said. "We're not joking, Mom. This dummy is evil. We said some secret words, and it came to life. We thought it was a joke, but—"

Their mom poked the dummy gently with her shoe again. Its arms flopped up, then down. The head bounced on the floor. The eyes didn't open. The dummy didn't move.

"I don't get the joke," Mrs. Harding said. "Could you explain to me what's funny here?"

"It's not funny," Vinny said. "It's real. We're not lying."

"The dummy is alive," Jonny added. "I swear."

Their mother let out a long whoosh of air. "I have a lot to do this morning. I don't have time for this silliness."

Vinny darted forward and picked the dummy up off the floor. Holding it around the waist, he started to shake it. "Move, Slappy!" he shouted. "Go ahead—move. Talk! Go ahead! Move!"

The dummy bounced limply in Vinny's hands. The head slumped forward, then back. The arms hung lifelessly at its sides.

"I don't know what your problem is," Mrs. Harding said, frowning. "But that dummy is definitely not alive. It's a few pieces of painted wood attached to a suit and tie. Dummies don't come to life, no matter how many magic words you say."

She turned and started toward the door. "Did you boys have nightmares or something last night?"

Vinny stood with the dummy still hanging limply between his hands. "Mom, listen to us—"

"No. I won't listen to any more," she replied. She stopped at the bedroom door. "Take that thing back to Ian. Right now. It's Ian's birthday gift. I'm not even going to ask you how it got here. I hope Ian loaned it to you two for a while. But now I want you to return it. Go ahead. Put on your shoes and carry it back to Ian's house."

She stepped out of the room, closing the bedroom door behind her.

As soon as she was down the hall, Slappy raised his head. He blinked his eyes. His red-lipped grin appeared to grow wider.

"Mom knows best, boys," he said.

28

A few minutes later, Jonny and Vinny left the house through the kitchen door. Vinny had the dummy slung over his shoulder. As he walked across the grass, Slappy's head banged against his back.

"*Stop bouncing me so hard,*" the dummy rasped. "*I can bite, you know.*"

The morning sun was still red and low in the sky. The grass was still wet from the early morning dew. They cut through their neighbor's yard and crossed the street.

"Ian is going to be surprised," Jonny murmured.

"*Ian is surprised that he has ten fingers!*" Slappy chimed in.

That made the two boys laugh.

"I like it when you pick on Ian instead of us," Vinny said.

"*You two are beneath me,*" Slappy said. "*You're*

a waste of my time. You're so dumb, you both stay up all night studying how to pick your nose!"

"Give us a break," Vinny muttered.

They ducked low behind a tall hedge and made their way along a narrow alley.

"Jonny," Slappy said. *"Do you know what you get when you put your brain into a dog's head? A really stupid dog. Hahahaha!"*

"Not funny," Jonny said.

"Not as funny as your face," Slappy replied. *"Is your face hurting you?"*

"No," Jonny said.

"Well, it's KILLING me! Hahahaha!"

They followed the alley to the end of the block. Hanging over Vinny's shoulder, Slappy's head bounced heavily against Vinny's back. Vinny held on to the dummy's legs with both hands.

Suddenly, the dummy pulled back one heavy shoe—and kicked Vinny hard in the stomach.

"Ohhh." Vinny groaned and doubled over. "Hey—what was *that* for?" he demanded.

"For fun!" Slappy replied. *"I like to get my kicks! Hahahaha!"*

Slappy turned to Jonny. *"Try to keep up. Do you take stumbling lessons after school?"*

Jonny mumbled something under his breath.

"Know what would help you be smarter?" Slappy asked him.

"No," Jonny said.

"I don't know, either! Hahaha!"

Vinny turned to his brother. "I wish we'd never kidnapped this jerk." They started to walk again. They waited for two SUVs to roll past, then crossed the street onto Ian's block.

The Barkers' red-brick house stood in the middle of the block, shaded by two leafy maple trees. Molly's silver scooter lay on its side near the driveway, gleaming under the morning sun.

"Boys, can you wave bye-bye?" Slappy said.

"Huh? What do you mean?" Vinny demanded.

"Bye-bye." Slappy gave Vinny another hard kick in the pit of his stomach.

Vinny gasped as pain shot through his body.

As he tried to catch his breath, Slappy slid off his shoulder. His heavy leather shoes hit the ground with a *thud*. And the dummy took off, running loose-legged but full speed across the corner yard.

"Bye-bye, dudes! Bye-bye!"

29

"Stop him!" Vinny groaned, still holding his throbbing stomach.

Jonny watched the dummy cross a driveway and continue his staggering run into the next yard. "Let him go. He's dangerous."

"No!" Vinny cried. He straightened up, took a few breaths, and started to chase after the dummy. He motioned with both hands for Jonny to follow him.

"We don't want Ian to know we stole him," Vinny explained. "If they find out we broke into their house last night and kidnapped the stupid dummy, we'll be in major trouble. We'll be doomed!"

Jonny realized his brother was right. He lowered his head and ran beside him, their shoes pounding the grass.

The dummy couldn't run fast. His legs were light and rubbery, and his big shoes were heavy. He ran awkwardly, like a newborn colt first testing how to trot.

Vinny raced up behind Slappy. He wrapped his arms around Slappy's waist and tackled him to the ground. Slappy's head hit the ground hard. Vinny landed on top of the dummy and pushed his face into the wet grass.

He grabbed both of the dummy's arms and twisted them behind his back. "Give?" Vinny demanded breathlessly. "Do you give up?"

Slappy spun his head around until it was completely backward. Then he raised his head—and bit Vinny hard on the nose.

Vinny screamed in pain and rolled off the dummy. He smoothed a hand over his nose, trying to wipe away the pain.

Slappy, his head backward, grinned up at him. But the dummy made no attempt to escape.

"Why did you do that?" Jonny demanded. He leaned over the dummy, hands on his knees. Ready to grab him if he tried to jump up and run away again. "Why did you run away from us?"

"*Uh . . . let me think . . . because I don't like you?*" Slappy replied. The dummy snickered. "*Actually, I thought you two slaves needed some exercise. It's not good that your stomach comes into a room before you do! Hahaha!*"

"No more jokes," Vinny said. "We're taking you to Ian. What more do you want?"

"*I want to get to that sheet of paper first,*" Slappy said. "*That's why I took off. Now let's get to business, slaves.*"

Vinny grabbed Slappy off the ground and swung the dummy back over his shoulder. "Ian can be your slave," he muttered.

"*You're ALL going to be my slaves!*" Slappy screamed angrily. "*You wouldn't want me to get another nosebleed all over you—would you?*"

Vinny shuddered. Once again, he pictured the smelly, hot glop that covered him and his brother, burning their skin and making their stomachs heave.

"Okay, okay," he said. "Jonny and I will look for that paper."

They stood in the neighbors' front yard, gazing at Ian's house. Sunlight filled the windows. They couldn't see inside.

"We've got one problem," Jonny said. "We don't want them to see us, right? We don't want them to know we're the ones who stole this creep."

Slappy, slumped over Vinny's shoulder, swung an arm and hit Jonny in the face with his wooden hand. "*Be polite. Don't call names, you moron.*"

"We could dump him on the front stoop and run," Vinny said.

"No. Not good," Jonny replied. "Someone in the living room might see us."

They both stared at the house.

"*Don't strain your brains, boys,*" Slappy said. "*Thinking is MAN'S work! And since you've never tried it before . . .*"

"I have an idea," Vinny said.

30

"Let's dump him in the garage and run," Vinny said.

They both turned their gaze to the square white garage at the back of the house. The garage door was closed, but they both knew Mr. Barker never locked it. Vinny gazed up and down the driveway. It was empty.

Did that mean the Barkers weren't home? Or was their car in the garage?

It didn't matter. This was the perfect place to hide Slappy and not be seen, Vinny decided.

"Sounds like a plan," Jonny told his brother.

"*Sounds like a lamebrain plan,*" Slappy chimed in.

The boys ignored the dummy. They crept along the side of the neighbor's yard, hunkering low behind a row of evergreen shrubs. Then they burst across the Barkers' driveway to the wide, white garage door.

Jonny grabbed the handle in the center of the door and began to pull it up. The door slid up easily. Halfway up, they could see Mr. Barker's blue Camry parked inside.

Vinny heard a sound and spun around. Had the kitchen door opened?

No. It must have been a tree branch creaking.

Breathing a sigh of relief, he ducked his head and carried the dummy into the garage.

Jonny followed him in. "Hurry," he whispered. "I hear music in the house. They're definitely home."

Vinny gazed around the garage. Shelves on the two side walls held tools and folded-up lawn furniture . . . bags of fertilizer and garden soil. A power mower stood against the back wall. A green garden hose was rolled up beside it.

"Here. This will work," Vinny said. He sat Slappy down on the trunk of the car and propped him against its rear window.

"*I don't like this,*" Slappy said, shaking his head from side to side. "*Sorry, slaves. I don't like this at all.*"

"Too bad," Vinny said. He gave Jonny a gentle push. "Let's get out of here."

"*Know what I do when I don't like something?*" the dummy rasped. "*Watch.*"

Slappy raised both hands in the air—and the garage door came slamming down.

"Hey!" Jonny uttered a startled cry. He and Vinny, inches away from the door, jumped back.

Jonny grabbed the inner door handle and tugged. The door wouldn't move. He tugged again. Then he turned to Slappy. "Let us out!"

Slappy tossed back his head and laughed his shrill, maniacal laughter. He raised his hands again and moved them up and down like an orchestra conductor.

Both boys ducked as garden tools came flying off the shelves. Steel hedge clippers sailed inches over Vinny's head and bounced off the side of the car.

"Whoa! Wait! Stop!" Vinny cried.

Slappy raised his hands. The garden hose unwound itself and began to spray a stream of water around the garage. The car horn began to honk. The power mower roared to life.

"Stop it! Stop it!" Vinny screamed.

Jonny strained and struggled with the garage door handle. But he couldn't get the door to slide up. A cold stream of water from the garden hose hit him in the back and made him scream.

The shelves on both walls were empty now. The tools had all come flying out. The heavy bags of soil and fertilizer slapped the hood of the car and slid to the garage floor.

Slappy waved his arms, conducting the horrible mess, grinning gleefully.

The horn honked and honked.

"Stop! Slappy—stop it!" Vinny pleaded.

And over the splash of the water, the roar of the power mower, and the pounding blare of the horn, both boys heard a shout—from outside the garage.

"Hey—what's going on in there?"

Mr. Barker.

Jonny turned to his brother. "We're in trouble," he said.

31

Slappy lowered his hands. His head drooped forward and he collapsed onto the Camry's trunk. The garden hose swooped to the floor. The mower and the car horn became silent.

A hush fell over the garage.

The two boys, drenched and shaking, watched in the sudden stillness as the garage door raised itself. Mr. Barker stood in a gray sweatsuit. He peered into the garage, and his eyes went wide with shock when he saw the chaos and damage.

"What on earth!" he cried.

"We didn't do it!" Vinny shouted.

"I—I don't believe this," Mr. Barker stammered. "Everything on the garage floor? Everything? It—it's all soaked!"

"I swear we didn't do it!" Vinny insisted.

Mr. Barker kept blinking and squinting. His face had turned bright red. He shook his head. "No . . . this is impossible."

"It wasn't us," Jonny said. "Vinny is telling the truth."

Mr. Barker turned to him, as if seeing him for the first time. He squinted from Vinny to Jonny, trying to focus.

"You two?" He finally managed to speak. "What are you doing in here? Why are you in the garage?"

"It's kind of a long story," Vinny said.

"We didn't do this. Seriously," Jonny repeated. "The dummy did it. We were returning it and . . . and it went crazy."

Mr. Barker turned to the car. He saw Slappy folded up on the trunk, his head down between his legs.

He gazed silently at the lifeless dummy for a long moment. "Guys, you're in a lot of trouble," he said finally. "We need to get your parents and have a very long talk. Look at my garage. Look at the incredible mess you made."

"But—" Vinny started.

Mr. Barker raised a hand, motioning for him to be quiet. "I hope you two can explain why you did this," he said, shaking his head again. "But I have a feeling you can't."

All three of them turned to the open door as Ian came running into the garage. "Hey—you found Slappy!" he cried. "Where was he?"

"Your cousins took him," Mr. Barker said,

speaking softly. "He didn't walk out on his own after all."

Ian gazed from Jonny to Vinny. "You took him?"

Vinny nodded. "It was . . . kind of a joke."

"The damage to my garage isn't a joke," Ian's dad said. "Sneaking into our house late at night and stealing something that belongs to Ian isn't a joke, either."

"It was just a prank," Jonny said. "We didn't mean any harm."

"You've done a lot of harm," Mr. Barker told him.

"But it was the dummy—" Vinny started.

Mr. Barker pointed to the dummy, still and lifeless, sprawled facedown on the car trunk. "You need a better story, guys. That one isn't going to work."

Mr. Barker stepped forward and lifted Slappy off the car.

"So, you see, Ian?" his father said. "You can relax now. It was your cousins. They took the dummy. The dummy isn't alive. Slappy is completely harmless."

Ian didn't reply. He knew the truth about Slappy. He knew his father was wrong.

All four of them left the garage and strode across the driveway toward the kitchen door. Ian was the only one who saw Slappy tilt his head and mischievously wink one eye.

32

It wasn't a happy morning in the Barker house. Mr. Barker had to call Jonny and Vinny's parents and tell them what their sons had done. They all had a long talk.

The Hardings agreed that the two boys would be grounded for a month. Jonny and Vinny had to promise to clean up the garage and make sure everything was put back where it belonged.

"And you have to stop telling dumb stories about Ian's ventriloquist dummy," Mrs. Harding added.

Jonny and Vinny grumbled to themselves. "Why doesn't anyone believe us?" Jonny asked.

"Because you're liars?" Molly said.

Mr. Barker backed the car down the driveway to make it easier for the two boys to clean the garage. Jonny and Vinny worked for an hour. They piled the garden tools back onto the shelves. They rolled up the garden hose and slid it back onto its holder. They worked for the rest of the morning. But there was still lots to do.

While the boys worked, Ian brought Slappy up to the attic. He locked him in a trunk and made sure the lock was tight.

They all had lunch together. Then Mr. Barker disappeared downstairs to his doll workshop to do some work.

The four kids stayed at the lunch table, having chocolate chip cookies for dessert. Molly sat at the head of the table, hugging Abigail to her chest. Vinny pointed at her half-eaten cookie. "Do you want the rest of that?"

Molly swiped the cookie out of his reach. "Of *course*. *You're* not getting it, Fat Face."

Vinny sighed. "Listen, can we have a truce? Seriously."

Molly eyed him suspiciously. "A truce? Do you even *know* what that word means?"

Vinny nodded. He lowered his voice. "The four of us have to stick together. We have to stop fighting all the time."

Jonny leaned over the table. His usual grin had disappeared. His face was pale and serious. "Listen to Vinny," he whispered.

"Your dad is wrong," Vinny said. "He's totally wrong about the dummy."

Ian squinted at him. He knew Vinny was right.

"You know as well as I do that Slappy is alive," Vinny said in a voice just above a whisper. "He messed up your garage. Jonny and I aren't that stupid. Why would we want to get ourselves in trouble? We didn't."

Molly laughed. "Are you trying to scare us?"

"You *should* be scared," Jonny told her. "Slappy is alive, and he's dangerous."

"I know you're telling the truth," Ian said finally. "At the talent show, Slappy said all those rude, horrible insults to everyone. I didn't. I didn't have any control over him. He . . . he was alive."

Molly hugged Abigail a little tighter. "If it's true that the dummy is alive, what are we supposed to do about it? Just leave him locked up in the trunk?"

"Maybe we should cut him in half or something," Ian said.

"No. No way," Jonny answered quickly. "He . . . he has powers. He can hurt you. He slimed Vinny and me. He burned us really bad."

"And you saw what he did in the garage," his brother added.

"So how can we be safe?" Ian asked, his voice just above a whisper.

Vinny tapped the tabletop tensely. "He told us what to do. He told us how to put him back to sleep."

"Huh?" Ian's mouth dropped open in surprise.

"He ordered us to find that slip of paper," Vinny said. "The one with the weird words on it."

"He doesn't want anyone to read those words out loud again," Jonny added. "Because that will put him back to sleep."

"And he wants to stay awake forever," Vinny whispered. "So he can make us all his slaves."

"Where *is* that paper?" Molly asked. "We had it down in Dad's workshop. Did you take it, Ian?"

Ian wrinkled up his face. "I don't remember." He shut his eyes, thinking hard.

"Maybe you left it downstairs," Vinny suggested.

Ian nodded. "Yes. Maybe I left it on Dad's worktable."

Vinny shoved his chair back, scraping the kitchen floor loudly. "Come on. Hurry, Ian. Let's go look for the paper."

Ian led the three others down the stairs to his dad's doll hospital.

Under a bright light, Mr. Barker leaned over a doll on his worktable. He had one hand pressed down on the doll. His other hand held a glue gun.

He turned in surprise when the four kids marched up to him. "Hey—what do you want?" He glanced at Molly. "Is Abigail broken again?"

She shook her head no.

Ian saw the sheet of paper immediately, on the corner of the worktable. "We need that paper," he told his dad. He made a grab for it.

To his surprise, another hand came from behind and grabbed for it, too.

Ian gasped and stared at Slappy. The grinning dummy pushed his way to the worktable. His glassy eyes were on the paper in Ian's hand.

"How—how did you get down here?" Ian stammered.

"Never mind!" Vinny shouted. "We have to read the words."

He grabbed the paper from Ian's hand and began to read: *"Karru Marri Odonna . . ."*

33

Before Vinny could finish, the dummy dove for
him. Slappy swung a big wooden hand up fast
and hard—and smashed it under Vinny's chin.

Vinny's eyes bulged. As pain swept through
his head, he started to choke. He grabbed
for his aching throat—and the paper flew out of
his hand.

Ian swiped at it, but Slappy got there first. The
dummy's hands moved fast. He ripped the sheet
of paper to pieces. They all watched the shreds
float to the floor.

Then Slappy tossed his head back, and his
laughter rang to the ceiling. *"I'm ALIVE!"* he
screamed. *"I'm alive FOREVER! Hahahaha!"*

Vinny was still rubbing his throat. Ian stepped
back from the gleeful dummy.

Slappy stood on the floor, raising his arms
above his head in triumph, and laughing his ugly
cackle of a laugh.

"Get ready to start your new lives!" he cried. *"Your new lives—as my SLAVES!"*

Pressing her hands to her cheeks, Molly let out a horrified cry and stepped back to the wall. Jonny had his eyes on the shreds of paper on the basement floor.

"This isn't happening," Ian muttered.

"I'm happening!" Slappy shouted. *"Don't just stand there like dummies. Say hello to your new MASTER!"*

"I don't think so," Mr. Barker said softly.

He grabbed the dummy in a tight arm-hold, wrapping his arms around him, holding him in place. "Quick, Ian!" Mr. Barker shouted. "Twist his head off. Hurry!"

Slappy thrashed and squirmed, but Mr. Barker held on tight.

"Let go! Let GO of me, slave!"

Ian raised both hands and took a step toward the struggling dummy. He hesitated.

"Grab it! Grab his head!" Mr. Barker shouted breathlessly. "Hurry, Ian. I can't hold him much longer. Hurry! Twist off his head!"

"Nooooooo!" The dummy let out a screech that rang off the low basement ceiling. He dropped hard, trying to duck out of Mr. Barker's hold.

Ian stepped close to the screaming dummy. His hands were trembling. His pounding heart sounded like thunder inside his chest.

Slappy ducked his head. Twisted his whole body. Tried to kick his captor.

Ian curled his hands around the dummy's neck.

"Now!" Mr. Barker cried. "Do it *now*, Ian!"

Ian took a deep breath and held it. Then he squeezed his hands tight around the dummy's wooden neck—and twisted his head off.

34

Mr. Barker let the dummy's body slide to the floor.

Struggling to catch his breath, Ian slumped against the worktable. He held Slappy's head in both hands. The eyes stared glassily at him. The wooden lips hung open.

Molly, Vinny, and Jonny didn't move. A hush fell over the basement.

And then the head between Ian's hands blinked its eyes. The mouth clicked as it slid up and down. And Slappy's head screamed in a shrill, furious rasp: *"YOU SHOULDN'T HAVE DONE THAT, SLAVES!"*

Ian screamed in horror and tossed the head onto the worktable. The head rolled, bounced against the wall, and stopped with its chin on the tabletop. Ian saw Slappy's body stand and begin to stagger, headless, around the basement.

Jonny and Vinny had backed up to the wall. Their faces were wide with fright. Molly, frozen in place, hugged Abigail in front of her, her eyes on the dummy head on the table.

"YOU SHOULDN'T HAVE! YOU SHOULDN'T HAVE!" the head screeched. *"NOW YOU HAVE TO PAY THE PRICE!"*

As everyone stared in shock, Slappy's body stopped its ragged wandering. It stood erect. It raised both hands in the air and waved to the shelves on the basement walls.

Silence.

For a long moment, nothing happened.

And then Ian heard a clattering sound.

A rustling, scraping sound. Soft thuds.

He saw movement. He gazed up at the shelves and gasped. "The dolls!" he choked out.

Everyone saw them now. The broken dolls were sitting up . . . standing . . . dropping off the shelves . . . hitting the basement floor with a clatter and a crash.

They were all moving. Sliding their arms and legs. Letting themselves drop from the shelves. Hitting the floor, then standing. Swinging their arms. Sliding their heads around. Testing themselves.

Alive. The dolls had all come alive.

Slappy's body stood with both hands raised. On the worktable, the head roared with maniacal laughter.

Ian stepped closer to his dad. The two of them watched the broken dolls move toward them. The

132

one-legged dolls . . . the armless dolls . . . the headless dolls . . .

Moving from all sides of the basement. Their feet clicking and scraping the floor . . . heads tilting and shaking . . . The ugly, broken dolls . . . hundreds of them . . . all staggering forward . . . Closing in on Ian, his father, Molly, and the two cousins.

Out of the corner of his eye, Ian saw Slappy's head bounce up and down excitedly on the worktable. It opened its mouth and cackled in triumph.

"Yes! Yes, my little doll slaves!" Slappy's head screamed. *"That's right. Keep coming. GET THE HUMANS! GET ALL THE HUMANS!"*

35

Ian screamed as the first doll attacked him. It was a tall boy doll, red hair, its eyes missing. Ian tried to kick it away. But it leaped above his shoe and grabbed on to the front of his T-shirt.

Two one-legged dolls scrabbled across the worktable and dove onto Mr. Barker's back. As he wrestled with them, a legless doll clung to his right leg with both hands. Another doll bounded onto his head and lowered itself over his face, trying to smother him.

More dolls came hurtling down from the shelves. The basement floor was covered with their ugly, broken bodies. They staggered and slipped and jumped forward, all silent, all moving toward Ian and the others. Slaves. Broken doll slaves. All following Slappy's orders.

Jonny and Vinny were down on their backs on the floor, wrestling with large cloth dolls. Molly kicked away a headless Barbie doll. But she was instantly swarmed over by three large, one-armed baby dolls.

The screams and cries of the humans were nearly drowned out by the scrape and clatter of the dolls as they attacked. And rising over all the sounds of horror were the cackling bursts of evil laughter from the openmouthed dummy head on the worktable.

And then, as Ian struggled to push a furry bear doll off his face, he saw Slappy's body stagger toward him. Ian heaved the bear doll across the basement. Two headless dolls clung to his knees, climbing up his legs.

Slappy's body slid past Ian. Its bow tie was still in place, even though its head was missing. The body stepped to the worktable, grabbed its head in both hands, and stuck it back in place on its wooden neck.

"Nooooo!" Ian screamed as two dolls shoved his legs from behind and he started to fall. His knees collapsed and he dropped to the floor on his back. Half a dozen more broken dolls swarmed onto him.

He kicked and thrashed. Tried to roll over. But they held him in place. A big blond bride doll sprawled over his mouth and nose. It pressed its white bridal gown down on his face. Ian struggled to breathe.

Suddenly, a voice rang out over the clatter and cried, *"STOP!"*

With a groan, Ian shoved the bride doll off his face. He pulled himself to a sitting position. He gasped as he saw Abigail—Molly's antique doll—leap from Molly's arms and stride across the basement floor.

Abigail jumped onto the worktable. *"Stop! Stop it—now!"* she cried in a squeaky, high voice.

The dolls continued to swarm the humans. Slappy, his head back in its place, moved quickly toward Abigail. *"Who ARE you?"* the dummy screamed angrily. *"How DARE you try to stop my doll slaves!"*

He made a grab for Abigail. But she slid out of his grasp.

With her delicate painted face and shimmery blue eyes, she turned to face him.

Her pale lips slid open. And her squeaky voice came out loud and clear as she shouted: *"Karru Marri Odonna Loma Molonu Karrano!"*

36

Slappy blinked a few times. Then his eyes snapped shut. His body folded in on itself. Slappy crumpled to the floor at Ian's feet, and his head fell off. Ian watched it roll to the wall.

Slappy's body didn't move. Sitting at the edge of the worktable, Abigail gazed down at it. She had a faint smile on her pale lips. Otherwise, her expression was blank.

The broken dolls all collapsed to the floor. They lay on their backs, their stomachs, their sides, lifeless and still. Jonny, on his back on the floor, lifted a large baby doll off his chest and heaved it across the room.

He stood up, breathing hard, his face red and sweat-drenched. He reached a hand down and helped Vinny to his feet. Vinny still had a doll wrapped around his shoulders. He shook his body and sent it clattering to the floor.

Ian stood close to his dad. They both gazed around the room, stared in amazement at the carpet of dolls over the floor . . . broken dolls that had come to life . . . that tried to kill them.

"We're okay," Mr. Barker said finally. A smile spread over his face. "We're okay."

And then, suddenly, they were hugging. A group hug. A celebration of their triumph. Slappy was asleep, no longer able to harm them. They hugged and laughed, and Mr. Barker had happy tears in his eyes.

He put an arm around Ian's shoulders and shook his head. "Ian," he said, "I guess Slappy wasn't the best birthday present I ever gave you. Don't worry. I'm going to lock him away where no one will ever find him."

"*Good*," said a voice behind them. Ian turned to see Abigail standing on the worktable. Her small hands pressed the sides of her old-fashioned gown.

"*Good*," Abigail repeated, now that all eyes were on her. *"I'm so tired of that dummy getting all the attention. Now, clean up this mess, slaves! Then bring me my lunch!"*

SLAPPY BIRTHDAY EPILOGUE

Slappy here.

Or what's left of Slappy.

Did you ever read such a tragic ending?

I'd cry my eyes out—but I'm trying to keep my *head*!

Who is in charge here? I'm very unhappy. And when Slappy is unhappy, Slappy gets revenge. Heads will roll!

Oops. Did I really say that?

Well, don't worry, slaves. I'll get myself together. And I'll be back soon with another Goosebumps story.

Remember, this is SlappyWorld.

You only *scream* in it!

This pirate will have you hooked!

ATTACK OF THE JACK!

Here's a sneak peek!

I sat on the edge of the seat and pressed my nose against the window glass as our bus bumped over the narrow road. A wooden sign came into view. It had a black ship's anchor across the top, above the words WELCOME TO SEA URCHIN COVE.

"We're here," I told my brother, Shawn.

He didn't look up from the *Battle Soccer* game on his phone. "I can smell the ocean," he said.

I pushed up the bus window. Yes, I smelled it, too. The air felt heavy and damp and smelled like fish and salt.

My name is Violet Packer, and I'm twelve, two years older than Shawn. Shawn and I had been to the ocean only once, five years ago on a family vacation. I was seven and he was five, and we were really excited to be there. But it rained every day, and we never got to swim or even play on the beach.

Now, here we were in this little seaside village, about to meet our Uncle Jim. Mom and Dad thought this would be a great summer vacation for us. We'd spend our time with Uncle Jim, and fish and sail and do whatever people who live on the ocean like to do. A whole new world for Shawn and me.

The bus slowed to a halt at the end of a row of low wooden buildings. Across the way, I saw a man with a thick black beard walking quickly along the storefronts, a heavy-looking fisherman's net rolled up on his shoulders. Two young women in shorts and sleeveless T-shirts stepped out of a small hotel named the Sail Inn.

I bumped Shawn with my shoulder. "Put the game away. We're here. Check out this cool village."

Shawn removed his earbuds and slid the phone into his shorts pocket. He's not like most little brothers. Shawn is very obedient. Mom said I was in charge this summer and, so far, Shawn had taken it seriously.

He isn't a pest like a lot of brothers. He doesn't tease me or try to start arguments or try to act like he's smarter. Actually, Shawn is very, very smart, but I don't think he has much of a sense of humor. He's quiet and serious, and doesn't really goof around.

He pretty much kept to himself during the long bus ride from Yellow Springs, Ohio. He read his baseball books and played sports games on his phone. The only time he got really excited and turned to stare out the window was when four cows started chasing the bus somewhere in Pennsylvania.

I think Shawn and I get along so much better than most sisters and brothers because we're almost total opposites.

I'm not shy or quiet. I like to talk and gossip and sing and laugh with my friends. I like a good joke, and everyone tells me I'm pretty funny. I get really excited about things, like this trip to Sea Urchin Cove to meet our Uncle Jim.

And I'm definitely not into sports like Shawn. I don't spend all my time watching ESPN and reading baseball novels and playing in Little League every weekend.

I'm tall and thin, and I've been taking ballet lessons since I was six. I love it, and my teachers say I'm a very promising dancer. Of course, I live in Yellow Springs, not New York City, where the great ballet schools are located. But Mom says if I'm still so devoted when I'm in high school, she'll take me to New York for auditions.

But right now I was in Sea Urchin Cove, and that was pretty exciting, too. *I'm about to start the most exciting summer of my life so far*, I thought.

About the Author

R.L. Stine's books are read all over the world. So far, his books have sold more than 300 million copies, making him one of the most popular children's authors in history. Besides Goosebumps, R.L. Stine has written the teen series Fear Street and the funny series Rotten School, as well as the Mostly Ghostly series, The Nightmare Room series, and the two-book thriller *Dangerous Girls*. R.L. Stine lives in New York with his wife, Jane, and Minnie, his King Charles spaniel. You can learn more about him at www.RLStine.com.

JACK BLACK
Goosebumps

BLU-RAY™ + DVD + DIGITAL HD

JACK BLACK
Goosebumps

FUNHOUSE

Goosebumps

"A frightfully fun flick for families."
-Peter Martin, *Twitchfilm.com*

Now on Blu-ray™, DVD & Digital

The Original Bone-Chilling Series

—with Exclusive Author Interviews!

NIGHT of the LIVING DUMMY
R.L. STINE

DEEP TROUBLE
R.L. STINE

MONSTER BLOOD
R.L. STINE

the HAUNTED MASK
R.L. STINE

ONE DAY at HORRORLAND
R.L. STINE

the CURSE of the MUMMY'S TOMB
R.L. STINE

BE CAREFUL WHAT YOU WISH FOR
R.L. STINE

SAY CHEESE and DIE!
R.L. STINE

the HORROR at CAMP JELLYJAM
R.L. STINE

HOW I GOT MY SHRUNKEN HEAD
R.L. STINE

SCHOLASTIC

www.scholastic.com/goosebumps

GBCL22

R. L. Stine's Fright Fest!
Now with Splat Stats and More!

THE ORIGINAL Goosebumps® BOOKS
WITH AN ALL-NEW LOOK!

R.L. Stine's Biography

REVENGE OF THE LIVING DUMMY
R.L. STINE

CREEP FROM THE DEEP
R.L. STINE

MONSTER BLOOD FOR BREAKFAST!
R.L. STINE

THE SCREAM OF THE HAUNTED MASK
R.L. STINE

DR. MANIAC VS. ROBBY SCHWARTZ
R.L. STINE

WHO'S YOUR MUMMY?
R.L. STINE

MY FRIENDS CALL ME MONSTER
R.L. STINE

SAY CHEESE - AND DIE SCREAMING!
R.L. STINE

WELCOME TO CAMP SLITHER
R.L. STINE